THE SOUL SNATCHERS

THE SOUL SNATCHERS

Richard Sanford

Inverness Press

Printed in the United States of America.

ISBN 978-0-9857445-3-3

Published by Inverness Press
Deerfield, Massachusetts
www.invernesspress.com

Everywhere the human soul stands

between a hemisphere of light

and another of darkness

Thomas Carlyle

People are strange when you're a stranger

Faces look lonely when you're alone

Jim Morrison

CHAPTER 1   TZARO

Tzaro Janssen shook his head as though shaking would clear it. A drink couldn't hurt either.

The Caltech satellite lab on Orcas Island overlooked the rolling metal sheen of Haro Strait. Inside at the front window, in his seat between computers and the bird's nest of monitors and cables that he called home, he was not seeing the undulating water or his screens. He needed to get real. A senior seismologist wasn't paid to daydream about a lost lady three thousand miles away. His job was to bear witness to uncertainties in the earth.

"Murray," Tzaro called over his shoulder, forgetting.

He rose groaning and crossed the hardwood floor, avoiding the cord covers, to the counter where Murray stood wide-eyed between the living room lab and the kitchen of the converted frame house.

"Murray, Murray," he said with a cadence of compassion, patting the simulated boy head. "Murray the moron now." The Gen 2 droid, a dozen years old, circa 2017, was good enough for government work, including table service, when he was operational. Even then his eyes, too huge, too blue, reminded Tzaro of anime.

"Dependent, little moron? Yes, I am hooked on you, hooked."

Tzaro took a pint tumbler from the dish drainer and pressed the mouth to the smoothie lip on the refrigerator front. Viscous strawberry undulated down. He savored the first, finest mouthful.

As he rounded the hapless android and headed back to his station, he corrected the miles. Not three thousand, he knew very well. Two thousand seven hundred by land, irrelevant anyway, and only two thousand one hundred some by air, Seattle to Atlanta. It amused him she wound up there. She was always edgier than that, but maybe Emory U was a draw. He pictured her at the front of a class of whatever journalism had become, but he really didn't know.

"Jesus Christ, never do that!"

The strawberry had almost cleared his head when the adrenalin hit. The screeching hundred-decibel alert was set to be audible anywhere in the building.

Tzaro clicked off the shriek, licked pink slop off the back of his hand, and peered into the screen. The alert came from the machine on his left, which reported the north seismometer, the last of the three triaxial broadband units sunk in the Salish Sea to do what it had just done—detect any action from the Fairweather or Hanning Bay faults to the Gulf of Alaska shear zone and the Aleutian megathrust. The epicenter was a fat red dot. Red and gold concentric rings spread outward with the P and S wavefronts. The jagged waveforms bunched into tight spikes in vivid colors. The highest amplitudes were fiery red, blending into magenta in the mid-range, darkening to blue at the flat baseline.

"Yes, yes, yes," he encouraged the little quakes to stay under moment magnitude MMS 3.0. He didn't need any of it at the end of Friday with one foot out the door. The primary event was finishing, but then there would be the secondaries. He needed to package all the data down to magnitude 1.0.

"Hey, buddy, what's the deal up there?" The voice came out of the speaker to his right. Caltech Seismo calling from Pasadena, the mother ship.

"Hey, Jerry. You picking it up?"

"Looks wimpy from here." Jerry was seeing summary data, fat samples.

"It's on Fairweather right at the coast. Could be two-eight, something like that."

"Gotta love the timing."

"No doubt. These little devils hijack my calendar and sync up. I can have it packaged in about thirty. I want to do some slicing on the main waves.

"And by the way, I put in the req for Murray's chipset over a week ago. He must have squealed to you guys a month or so before he went down, right? How would you like deteriorated capacity—"

"Okay, daddy, okay. Got you covered. Your chipset went out today. You'll get texted, then droned."

"Copy. Catch you later."

Tzaro watched the waves spike and flatten. It would be a while.

He stood facing the window and the smooth water beyond. He remembered when it was all on track. He had both hands on the wheel. He had a career that made sense, a family, and the smugly termed "lifestyle." Checking his reflection on the plane of glass, he wondered which lines traced that history and which mapped to his current coordinates on a fault line between women, one nearly his student, the other suspended in memory. His dark eyes looked haunted and too intense. His hair seemed to extend the theme—black curls, electric twists, fewer by the day. What would she think if she saw him now?

How long since they had been together? The year of her New York move. She had her first reporting job, covering that Senate race in Ohio, the ex-figure-skater. They had rendezvoused in Cincinnati. That was the last time. Seventeen years. At some point in their communications she had mentioned an exotic, something with an "a," Armenian or Azerbaijani, when that was trendy for young ladies prepped at Groton or Phillips Exeter. He had met Lauren a year later and the rest was the rest, the fate he chose, the settled mode—basically, his mistake. One he could never undo.

He imagined she married the guy. She had a daughter, he knew that, a year younger than Derek. They had mailed a few times and she had seemed warm but reticent. He knew it was the A-A. A swarthy and tireless humper he was, no doubt, with two penises. When the conventional one flagged, he cut over to the backup.

He needed to get a grip. When he started this, he could spiral.

> The dizzying brightness, low October sun on a pure day. Nothing else memorable about Cincinnati but that downtown park because of her. On her new job, covering the Senate race as meaningless now as it was hot then, in the days of high aspirations. On the path in front of him, turning back, squinting smile, dark hair in a dazzling aurora. The light crush of her curls in his fingers.

The fourth event started. It was down to amplitude four, MMS 1.3. Hints of magenta at the tips of tiny spikes.

Two screens to the right caught his eye. Silent CNN was showing a lone reporter on a subway platform with the caption, "London Tube Ridership Down 30%." He punched up the sound.

"A CNN poll bears out the findings of the London Transit Commission. It should be noted that a majority of those polled declined to respond. Of those who did, nearly forty percent able to walk to their destinations preferred to do that, up to three kilometers. Almost ten percent preferred to pay London taxi or ride fares. Both groups stated the most important factor to them was the ability to travel alone.

"Similar declines in the use of subways and light rail are being seen in metropolitan areas in the United States, including New York, Washington, D.C., and San Francisco. Ridership on all forms of public transit is down in other densely populated metro areas including Mexico City, Hong Kong, and Seoul."

The shot cut to a new story—a sidewalk ganged with squad cars, volleys of red and blue lights hitting a two-story stucco apartment building. The video was amateur, probably phone. Officers had a cuffed white man by both arms and his belt, stocky in a black Corona T-shirt, bending him into a car.

"Police in San Diego have made an arrest in the fourth case of lethal domestic violence in that city in a week. At this time the cases do not appear to be related. In a press conference yesterday, Chief of Police Tamara Cruz stated no motive had been identified for any of the crimes."

"Poppin' off in paradise," Tzaro said absently to the air, trying to maintain indifference. But the combined effect of the two stories had him on edge. The feeling was oddly familiar, an undercurrent, dark and unsettling.

He heard the door.

"Hey." Therica looked gloriously winded, bike helmet in hand.

"Hey. Warm out there?"

She stuck out her tongue. Therica Lundy was a solid young woman with a ring-a-ding smile, younger than he by an even decade. He wasn't usually attracted to redheads, but he knew this one would be trouble from the start. A sailor-striped tank top, nicely muscled legs in cargo shorts, one pagan inklet below her calf—resistance had been futile. Overall, Therica projected a healthy heartland summer look, although she hailed from northern California, Eureka.

Tzaro rounded off his moment of admiration by reminding himself, not for the first time, that a man in his early forties with an advanced degree and a divorce behind him should know better. Too late for that one.

"You want that?" She was looking at the smoothie he had only started.

"No. Sure, go ahead."

She took a swig.

"What have we got here?" She was checking his screen.

"Fairweather Friday. It's about over, but it was a beaut, granular. You'll see."

"How much more..." She read the legend and answered herself. "This is event six."

"Jerry just called. I told him I'd package it tonight."

"Will you show me?" She meant all of it, the twenty minutes of replay. As inspiring as her form was her enthusiasm.

"That's what I'm here for."

Therica had been hooked by local history, the 7.2 off Cape Mendocino that had rocked her hometown in 1992. She had gone back to school for her seismo masters and was happy to land the low-paying assistantship in her field. The lab in the San Juans was regarded as a plum.

She brushed her palm across the back of his head and he relished the stroke. What else could he do? It was where things were now, wherever that was.

He refocused on the screen, assessed the dwindling spikes, and cut them off. If Jerry needed more—he wouldn't need more, by definition. Tzaro clicked, and the waveforms skated into reverse.

Off to his right, he heard volume rising.

"...are expected in north Moran State Park tomorrow." She had switched to local news.

"Listen, this is about..."

He knew full well what it was about.

"Orcas Island police presence is expected to be normal with no additional support from the other islands. Although it's officially a protest demonstration, event organizers are

expecting a festival atmosphere, with musical performers on
two stages—"

"Don't you love that? How they trivialize—"

"Lighten, perhaps. 'Life is far too serious not to be taken
lightly.' Who said that?"

"Not so light for people who are losing their homes."

"British author, twentieth century."

"I forgot, you were an English major once, weren't you?"
Her recall came with a twist of disdain. "You think it's a joke."

"I think it has potential for humor. Just before this there
was a story about people who preferred total isolation to riding
public transit—ready to deplete their savings to avoid human
contact. I'm just saying criticality is relative."

He clicked off the reverse in the flat wave, back in the time
before domestic conflict.

"Did you want to see this?" he tried.

"You don't like that Morgan's coming."

"Not at all. Any friend of yours…It's fine, it's fine.

"Lawrence Durrell," he added with a grin, looping back to
his quiz question, aglow with geniality. "You want to see?"

"After you package it," she said, too cool, back turned. She
clicked off the news and went to the diagonal corner of the
room, to the armchair with the end table. She rooted in her
backpack and he saw her phablet come out.

He started the S wave analytics and tried to concentrate on
running the job, the downside of auto jobs being that they
were auto and there was no point in concentrating on them.

He glanced back to the corner, trying to gauge her annoyance. She had put on her glasses, the better to see her screen,
and was tapping intently. Her glasses always did it to him—
the affiliation of studious girl with hiker girl. He was fairly
confident she wasn't doing it to be irresistible. But he didn't
like the way her face changed when she focused on the screen,
as though she had gone into, and away.

"Is that Ping?" he said. Two seconds. No response. Three.
"Is that Ping?"

"Wundrus," she said without looking up.

He knew she was thinking he was a relic because he wasn't into Ping, Wundrus, Uptake, or any site, mashup, or other entity that smacked of social networking.

"Luddite," she said out of nowhere. At least she was finally looking at him.

"I'm selectively Luddite."

She grinned. Relief had been hard won but he'd take it. He could go back to wave analytics in peace, and she could return to Wundrus.

He didn't understand how he could simultaneously feel old in present company and like a teenager mooning over a ghost of the past a coast away. That problem he could identify. But he had no way to understand, or anticipate, that in the space of twenty-four hours, Therica would be someone he did not know.

CHAPTER 2   THERICA

Tzaro and Therica stood on the pedals, cruising around the last corner before the house. On the ride from the lab they had stuck to the bike trail, cool in the shade of tall cedars, a welcome respite in the last days of August. As he often did, Tzaro consciously tried to ignore the absurdity of the knee-high white picket fence. It suited the yellow frame house, white trim. He would never have chosen either—high contrast to the three thousand square feet of his SoCal days. But it was reasonable for a two-bedroom rental on the island, although now he was rethinking the second bedroom, which had enabled the current situation. If he could blame anything for stumbling into the topic he had successfully avoided for the fifteen-minute ride, it would be the second bedroom.

"They're Warwicks, right?" he said.

"Eighteen hundred of them, "she said, loosening her helmet. At the hitching post at the corner of the house, they took out their locks.

He imagined the squadron of alien programmers, referred to by the name of their agency—the first of the outsourcers to shuttle in developers from outside the solar system.

"They're going to be taking over Beacon Hill and—"

"Columbia City, yeah I know."

"You think the demonstration is silly, don't you? A lot of people who've lived there for years are going to be—"

"Highest and best use," he said. "It's inevitable." He sounded like a jerk, he knew. He was surprised at himself, but if pressed, he knew very well why he was down on the subject, and the protest. She went right for it.

"You don't want Morgan to stay here, that's what this is about."

"This what?"

"You know what I mean. Your attitude. You said it was fine with you. Remember?"

"I said it *after* you asked her."

"Okay, fine. She can stay with me."

He flashed on her studio with a futon bed, a poor match for his picket fence palace. She was retightening her chin strap.

"She can stay, all right? I wouldn't want to interfere with this moment of historical import. But please, next time can we discuss these things first?"

"We did discuss it. You have no memory of it. And the next time, you can discuss it with yourself." She turned the bike and drove the pedal down. Already she was back on the street.

"Hey. Jeez Louise."

His was an ancient Trek mountain bike from an Alibaba ad. Therica was on her beloved carbon fiber Fuji Redondo. By the time he turned back onto the street, she was halfway down the block.

This is a volatile and feckless child, he thought. A fistful of quills. But that reminded him of his hands on her, hands full, both hands.

She was on the Adams straightaway and there were cars, just enough that he didn't want to keep shouting after her. She wasn't going full speed, just fast enough to make him toil. By raising the topic, he had put distance between them. Did he have a diabolical intention? Yes or no, it was up to him to close it. Wasn't this the relationship story of his life? It seemed familiar.

"Can we talk?" he blurted six feet behind her. "Can we—!"

She angled away, braked.

He braked.

"You know," he gulped, "I have nothing. Against. Your friend. Enthusiast—crusader for the rights of all. Okay? The house makes sense. She's already coming to the house." He felt sweat popping from all glands and pores.

Therica surveyed him from her position of strength, imperious. Her jaw was set, but he detected a hint of softening around the eyes.

"Can we go back now?" he said. What was she waiting for, *please*? There was a sparkle of sweat on her upper lip, and he picked up a musky warm drift of her skin cream.

"I know why you're saying all this," she said.

It was the first time she had hit him, and it was perfect. They had just made the bedroom. The striped tank top had been praying on his mind, and on any normal day, their tops would have come off first. But on this special day, supercharged, it was her shorts and his jeans. He had felt the whack as he dropped his briefs. She was working out their spat in the most creative way. The sting worked on all levels, and he was happy to return the favor.

She popped the top over her hair and let it drop to the floor. Tzaro admired Therica's southern hemisphere, its balance and proportion, but under interrogation he would have to admit it was her top that inspired and awed him like beacons of a new world, but taut and heavy in his hands when he weighed them from behind.

In the bedroom of thick, grainy evening light and shadows, they hit the sheet in a sweaty tangle. He got in a salty lick, like a lingering taste of summer.

They rolled over, and when she ground against him and he asked her to raise both arms, hands behind her head, a favorite of his, Tzaro thought of seismic waves. In their training sessions she had watched him freeze and label the peaks of P waves with such perfect focus, the same concentration she was bringing to their zone of union.

On their sides in the half light, her breasts together so he could span them with his hand, he was filled with a sense of praise for all her tawny places, crevices of divine intervention, crevices crepuscular! His eyes swept over her with wanderlust, their bodies concatenated in a scissors. In their final pounding race, he was where he longed to be, out of himself.

It was only in the shower that his unwelcome self caught up with him. He thought of the waves again, but this time of the tiny ones that had gone undetected, slipped under his marriage, minute shearings that spread until they split it.

He thought of Therica's name, how when she first told him he thought she was joking. It was a short form of the United States of America, and it went back to her great grandmother whose parents were Irish immigrants inspired by the wonders of the New World. Solid colleen she was, of solid stock, smart and ambitious. And with a healthy appetite and enthusiasms skin-on-skin. What a great wife, he indulged in the cliché while drying off, she would make some man. But he was still clearheaded enough to remind himself it would not be him.

She had beaten him out of the shower and was sitting on the edge of the bed in her white nightshirt, hair wet, focused on her phablet. He slipped in beside her. Her throat smelled like coconut and sun.

"What's for eats?" He put his arm around her. Thumbnail heads and message boxes crowded her screen. He fantasized yanking her out of place and sweeping her away, underarm carry.

"I could make enchiladas," she half-offered.

"We have salmon Mixer-Lot left, don't we? I can make it."

"You're so sweet," she said into the bedroom air.

He headed for the kitchen. Give my love to Wundrus, he did not say.

"Five," he did say, and Channel 5 News bloomed on the TV.

"…sixteen-year-old girl in custody."

Chopper footage was showing an upscale two-story house triangulated with arcing streams from five truck hoses. White smoke clouded most of the building, but a patch of orange flame sucked at a corner. The legend at the bottom of the screen read, "Teenage girl torches home. Parents and child trapped inside."

"We are seeing a live stream from Bethesda, Maryland. As we reconstruct this story from less than an hour ago, fire prevention responded to a report of a house fire in this affluent neighborhood. When firefighters arrived, the building was completely engulfed, and all efforts have been focused on protecting the other homes in the area. Police apprehended a sixteen-year-old girl who is reported to have set the fire. Her parents and possibly her fourteen year-old brother are thought to be inside—"

"Seven," he said.

"…interrogating the sixteen-year-old girl who is being held in this case—"

"Forty-four." CNN too.

"…here in Bethesda, Maryland. And now we go to Washington, D.C., where Dr. Kenneth Elston, professor of psychology at Georgetown University, is joining us. Dr. Elston is the author of *Frenzy: The Genesis of Crowd Mind.* Dr. Elston, the details of this case are just emerging, but there seem to be similarities to recent incidents in Newcastle, England, and Cologne, Germany, where homes were consumed and lives lost in fires set by a family member. There have been reports that the suspects arrested seemed to be in a trancelike state."

"You should check this," Tzaro sent in the direction of Therica on the bed, head down. Silent tapping.

"Or not."

"...individual in the Newcastle event, a schoolteacher in her thirties, was under the care of a psychotherapist..."

Tzaro migrated to the kitchen, liberated the leftover salmon and vegetable mix, and popped a Hop Valley IPA.

"...consistent with a family of disorders such as schizoid personality disorder or..."

He sipped the brew absently and pondered. These stories, which had been surfacing in the media for weeks, seemed to be gaining something like critical mass. News sites crackled with a wealth of small horrors. The blogosphere post-processed.

"... a social dimension, which is defined now as much by our virtual communities..."

These people. What was the thread? he wondered, the commonality. Fleeing strangers, kids turning on loved ones. Was it discoverable?

He took two more small swigs, which brought perspective on the suffering world.

He ducked back into the refrigerator, pleased to see that two salad packs remained. He peeled back the tops and was ready to mic salmon Mixer-Lot when motion, or the ghost of motion, caught his eye.

A figure was standing at the open door, outside the screen. At first it was a black silhouette, medium height, with a backpack hump. The obvious had not fully dawned on him in the next second when the doorbell rang. The bell triggered the porch light, and the figure bloomed to life as though materializing on a stage. She squinted in the sudden brightness, backpack strap over one shoulder, dark cropped hair and a headband, commando pants and ankle boots, looking ready for war.

CHAPTER 3   MORGAN

"How do you stop a bus?" Tzaro tossed it out to no response. "I heard you froze Google cold in the Tenderloin. I have images of superheroes." Antediluvian, he realized. He sounded antediluvian.

"You give the driver a choice. He can keep going and lose his job and his license and face criminal prosecution, or he can stop."

Morgan wasn't quite what he had expected. She was Therica's age—they had been roommates at UC San Francisco—but she seemed younger. Her voice had a chirpy edge, and she was lean and taut with visible cheekbones. A turbocharged metabolism, he guessed, wondering what she ate. For their dinner they were supplementing the salmon and salad with apple slices, Gouda, and crackers, plus three Hop Valley IPAs, his second.

"I think it was so gutsy," Therica said. "Deep down we all wonder if we could do something really flagrant like that, lie down in front of a bus. If we believed in something enough..."

"It took courage, absolutely," Tzaro said, having trivialized a work of social responsibility, executed unflinchingly in a moment of truth. "So San Francisco was about Google moving into the Tenderloin. And Therica tells me it's Warwicks in Seattle, eighteen hundred—"

"The Mesmark complex will go on Beacon Hill with a satellite campus in Columbia City." She was watching him with assessing gray eyes. "They want to put their housing right there. For those who aren't directly displaced, obviously rents will rise. City council estimates ten percent, but we know from experience it's more like double that. For people making minimum wage, it's an impossible situation. So there will be more homeless, which will hit services that are already underfunded. Their shelter will be appropriated by developers. But we can stop it. It's our responsibility to stop it."

Morgan on a roll was a force, wired and wiry. He imagined her scaling a cell tower to plant a charge, knife in her teeth.

Sure is strange

You got to pick up every stitch

It was his choice, coming from the old Advent speakers and the country before they all were born. He preferred the music of his parents, a previous kingdom on earth.

Morgan and Therica went on to their families. He could see them as a duo thrown together in college, first imagining Therica as lead and Morgan as sidekick but then seeing Morgan flipping her natural pagan hair of the day over her shoulder and leaning in to make her point, the vein prominent in her neck. She was too spirited to play a bit part.

Tzaro watched them chatting like roommates. He knew from Therica that Morgan's hometown was outside Lincoln, Nebraska, which explained her escape to the Bay Area. She had also told him Morgan was bi, which fit his original picture, and he imagined that translated to NA. But he had to admit her spark was not unattractive.

Beatniks out to make it rich

And what did she think of him? He was the older man. What had Therica really told her, besides the sanitized version she had told him? Maybe she had painted him as Mr. Right. He was getting up.

"I've got 'em," he said. He started collecting dishes, stacking them on his palm like a robot. He was a middle-aged, divorced robot with a suspect chipset.

"What's the plan?" he slipped in. "For tomorrow. When do we leave?"

Therica checked him. Her look said *we*?

"People will be coming in tonight," Morgan said, "staying in the park. The jam starts at eleven, so whenever before that. Hey," she said, nodding, "solidarity," and grinned.

In the presence of female solidarity, he accepted that the proper place for him was on the margin. As he fed plates into the washer conveyor, he heard occasional flurries of laughter.

"He was a jerk." It was Therica's voice.

"Who you couldn't get enough of."

"I was not obsessed!"

"You were totally obsessed."

By the time he returned to the table they were gone, down the hall to Morgan's room.

He could hear them chirping along, girls at a sleepover. The easy goal was the bathroom and a shower. When he reemerged, the tone had changed. Quieter, but not intimate.

"Hey, you spaced or what?" It was Morgan's voice.

"No, what? What?"

"Nothing."

"Nothing is nothing." Something in her tone, mildly unnerving. He had heard it before recently.

Silence. He went from eavesdropping to bed. His thoughts went as they often did, to Lauren, thoughts he tried to block while wishing no ill will, and then to Derek. He would be heading back to international school in a little over a week. Their next call would be Sunday.

Then, inevitably, he was across the country, a diagonal beam of connection, whether the one connected to knew it or not. Somehow she was always with him.

At some point he rolled over. He tested Therica's side of the bed—flat and cool against his arm. Across the hall he saw the bathroom door outlined with an odd light. He recognized the emanation, its composite of colors and brightness. She was on her phablet. Mailing some guy? Some avatar her age? If so, he thought, "okay" was the only answer. He had his own dreams. He took a deep breath, exhaled deliberately, and rolled over. He needed sleep for solidarity morning.

CHAPTER 4   SCREEN GRAB

"I was in there like ten minutes last night, fifteen at most," Therica said. "Is that permissible?"

Tzaro picked up a strong whiff of falsehood. He held the button down and the coffee grinder burred.

"I just needed to unwind," she finished. She was clenching a juice glass.

"I missed you," he said pleasantly, but she was turned to the cabinet pulling glasses.

"It's under a mile, right?" Morgan had joined them, undetected, in the kitchen. A glass clacked over on the tile counter.

"Hey, sorry, I scared you." Morgan touched Therica's shoulder, and Tzaro noticed her stiffen.

"No, no problem, I...Is O.J. okay? Frozen not squeezed, I'm afraid. We have granola, oatios. I remember you don't like eggs."

"Either is fine. What can I do? Morning," she added to him.

"Good morning. And right, under a mile to the park, maybe twenty minutes on foot. Coffee? Good, it's on the way."

Morgan's hair was wet from the shower, and she had changed to a loose black top with white Japanese characters. Tzaro thought karate, but maybe she was only projecting an image, tough by association. She took to slicing strawberries and bananas.

While they ate at the counter, his focus was on Therica. Morgan was ranting mildly about immigration rights and why, for the protection of immigrants, they did not apply to Warwick aliens. Therica said little, lingering in the corner where she had set out the glasses. She was nodding along, but it was clear to him her attention was elsewhere. At one point she excused herself.

"She seems different," Morgan said matter-of-factly.

"I've noticed it too—it isn't you. I bet she's thinking about her review, which I write. How's that for a vote of confidence?"

Morgan grinned, looked down, up, away.

To his surprise, Therica returned, chatty, phablet in hand. She and Morgan resumed, on the demonstration this time, and Therica powered the device on. Tzaro migrated to the coffeemaker beside her, not because he needed coffee but because it was beside her, so he could do what he had never considered doing before.

Tzaro waited in the bedroom until they were ready at the door.

"I'll catch up. Murray's new board is going to the lab and I don't want to leave it there."

He and Therica hugged and he watched the two until they turned out of sight at the end of the block. Therica had done as he had hoped. He went to the table and picked up her phablet.

He pressed the power button and waited for the prompt. His insides were clenching. He tapped and the keyboard opened.

s-y-z-1-9-9-1

What you entered was not recognized.

He was sure he had caught the first part over her shoulder. *Syzygy*, one of her favorite words.

S-y-z-1-9-9-1

What you entered—

"Shut the fuck up!"

He replayed the patterns of her fingertips. She didn't shift at first, it was later.

s-y-z-1-9-9-!

"Yes!"

Therica's home screen opened in his hands—a dock on an empty lake, idyllic. Eureka, or a stock shot.

So far so good. The real test remained. He tapped the Wundrus icon. The Login button was upper right.

"Yes!"

Her username, "Ther," was prefilled. He tapped the Key box.

The login dialog opened—not even an iris scan, pupil alignment only.

He entered the syzygy-inspired characters one by one.

"Thank you, thank you." He appreciated her steady-headed normalcy, using the same password against all advice.

That was all he needed. He left the sophomoric splash screen of Wundrus open with its floating heads, grabbed his smart badge, and was through the door and into the old silver Tesla he had spent a fortune on maintaining but couldn't forsake. The back of his shirt was soaked with sweat. He leaned forward to air it out and gunned it.

In the lab he rummaged furiously through the hardware on the shelves. He knew a Turbo Core reader was there somewhere, and he was right. The packet compressor enabled Spokestream to Captor. He connected her phablet to a spoke and the Captor screen opened on Wundrus.

He raised the frame rate to thirty-two per second and tapped Start. He let Captor grab screens for a full minute before he stopped the sequence. Then he punched up the first dozen of two thousand images on the MagRes monitor and started to page through. What he wanted began on page three, frame image twenty-seven. It was front and center in image twenty-eight. By twenty-nine, it was gone.

As he stared into the image, inspecting every detail, he eventually realized he had stopped breathing. His heart was doing a hard flutter.

Duration, a sixteenth of a second. He forwarded another full second, thirty-two frames. The image again, two frames. That was enough. He pulled a bubble memory pastille from a drawer and backed up the two-thousand-image output.

Shut down, disconnect. Turbo Core back to the shelf. He wanted to leave it all as it had been. Nothing else was.

CHAPTER 5   BREAK-OUT

Tzaro was almost to Moran Park when he realized the bubble memory was still in his pocket. He had meant to stash it in the back of his drawer when he returned Therica's phablet to the dining room table as she had left it, rotated twenty degrees left. His head had been swimming with the images of her screen like cards in a game he had no idea how to play.

He was past the parking lot, striding as fast as he could on the road already crowded with walkers and bikers. Spiked hair and ink were standard, but he saw a white-haired couple biking—the man in a vintage Mariners T-shirt. A shirtless skateboarder veered past him and weaved expertly down the blacktop. Tzaro could hear thrumming of congas in the park and he followed it in.

Through an entrance flanked by tall firs and cedars, the park opened on a crowd of milling visitors, many armed with signs, homemade and printed. *Save Freakin' Hill. Columbia*

City for People. Stop War on the Poor. The air felt charged. Two Orcas police stood casually on the margin of the crowd.

"Sorry." He shoulder-bumped someone. A guy in guerilla face paint, red and white, swung around and then marched on. He was heading toward a stage on the perimeter of the clearing where a clump of spectators pumped fists in the air. Phones were out, their owners tapping shots. Two drones hovered above them. Petty intimidation? Tzaro wondered. Or could be news, anything licensed. Tzaro's phone was in its usual resting place in the glove compartment. He scanned the crowd for Therica.

"Small world."

Tzaro had been so focused, he was unaware that he and the towering figure had been drifting together. For a second he blanked on the name, although he knew the tall Indian perfectly well. He was one of the few people he met when he first came to the island.

"Hey-hey, Wilson!" He clasped the meaty hand.

"What's happening? How's your Model X?"

At six foot one, Tzaro didn't often find himself looking up in a conversation, but he did with Wilson, who had him by three inches and at least sixty pounds.

"No problems. I've become a lousy customer. How's biz?"

"No kidding." Wilson sounded gruff but he was grinning. He wore his hair tight in a ponytail, and one high cheek had a chip, like a badge of growing up on an old prison camp reservation. His T-shirt had a native design, raven or bear. Tzaro tried to remember his tribe, maybe Tulalip. "Besides you, good."

Tzaro always appreciated about Wilson that his specialty was gas combustion, mechanical. Volvo, Merc, BMW, the classics. When he saw the Tesla, he said sure, it had to happen someday.

A cheer went up in front of the stage, and the crowd pumped their signs. Wilson's danced the highest. *Stop War on the Poor.*

"You're sympathetic to the cause," he added.

"Why not. It's my girlfriend, a friend of hers..."

"She's right. Stop it now. You let land grabs happen, you wind up 'indigenous people'."

"Morgan!" Tzaro shouted across the crowd to the right side. "Hey, there's one of them. Later," he said to Wilson and started heading toward her. But something was off. He expected them both to be in the middle, around the stage.

"Hey!" He caught her eye and waved, but she didn't wave back.

"She took off." Morgan was not her inscrutable commando self. He saw a new tightness around her eyes. "We came in. There were people handing out signs, Therica took one. We were... she just dropped it... I thought she was going in on her own. I picked it up and she was gone. Like she just vanished."

He felt a grip in his chest like confirmation. The news stories from those other places were coming home.

"How did she, what did she seem like? Was she all right?"

Her face said it all. She was glancing around furiously.

"There?" she said.

She was squinting past the middle of the crowd and the stage toward the far border of the clearing.

Tzaro started toward the figure. Therica, definitely, the top she wore, her hair. Then he was jogging, dodging protesters who drifted aimlessly, backing into his path. She was nearly at the line of trees.

"Sorry." He bumped a guy, pirouetting absurdly to miss his girlfriend.

He lost her. He was feeling sick, breath tightening. He kept on in the same direction. Picked her up again. She was leaving the clearing, heading into the trees.

The crowd was behind him then and he was running hard. An apron of ferns and ivy spread out before the firs. That was where she had been standing. She had disappeared into the forest.

"Therica!" he shouted.

"Therica!" came from behind him. He hadn't been aware of Morgan following. She looked sweaty and out of focus. His left contact had slid to the outside of his eyeball. He knelt to constrain the drop zone if he popped it out into the ivy. He was panting and sweating, working his eyelid with his finger, trying to mash the plastic back into place.

"Therica!" Morgan called again, beginning to work her way into the woods.

It seemed to center. Tears welled, floating the contact into a blur. He blinked, trying to focus.

"Hey hon," he heard ahead of him. "You okay?"

He scrambled to his feet, and as he joined Morgan, Therica was blurred but clear enough. She was crouching, thighs tight, ready to bolt.

Tzaro blinked furiously to clear his eyes, not quite believing what he saw. Therica's hair was part up, part straggling over one shoulder. She was giving him a probing look, as though seeing him for the first time, stripped of fantasy and good intentions, any wishful idea of who he was or where they were going. And not probing only but wary, mistrustful, betraying animal fear.

"Hon, it's okay," he said. "I know what the problem is. You're going to be okay." He and Morgan began to move toward her, and he extended a hand.

"Stop!" she spat and they froze. "You don't know anything. Get away from me!"

Therica took a step backward. Her heel caught a root and she lurched sideways and went down.

CHAPTER 6   WHEN THE RAIN CAME

Triggered, no resistance possible, Tzaro crashed forward and dropped beside Therica, clutched her bare arm.

First it was the scrambling under him in a blur, and then his wrist and hand. Together, they jammed the senses. She had caught the back of his hand with her nails like claws. A woman who had trusted his every touch was like a red-fanged animal scrabbling away from him with the velocity of pure fear.

"Hey don't...!" Morgan called somewhere behind him.

His solid insides, with reliable heart and stomach, were hollowed out. Tzaro could only watch Therica flee, stunned by the power of her affliction and the useless knowledge that he had an idea of the cause but no cure. Vaguely he became aware of blood rising from three rakes on his hand.

Morgan was past him. He scrambled up and followed.

Therica was out of the woods, into open field. Fifty yards in front of her stood another perimeter of trees, either more forest or a wooded strip before the road.

Tzaro had hit full stride and he was breathing hard, so when he heard it first, he wasn't sure. But in the next second he saw Morgan slow and turn in the direction of the sound, and Therica did the same.

A few of the demonstrators were starting to run. The burr he had heard like a vague echo flooded over the trees. Two black helicopters hovered above the tree line behind the stage, low enough to whip the grass. Over the open field, the whack of the blades turned to thunder.

The core of the crowd in front of the stage dropped their signs and began to scatter, most in the direction of the park entrance. The choppers hovered for a moment then nosed out, crossed paths, and hooked over the far woods. In a long moment they seemed to hang suspended, then they banked and turned and bore down on the crowd in the bottleneck.

Out of the sky, chariot wheel, Tzaro flashed absurdly. Apollo's chariot wheel was off. One of the drones was on them sideways like a huge metal discus. It hit behind Morgan and rolled insanely, careening over the grass. She was down.

He dropped beside her, clutched her arms.

"You alright?"

"Yeah, yeah, I'm okay. What the fuck?" The choppers were thunderous. They heard screams.

At the far end of the clearing, green spray was dropping from one of the helicopters, fanning into a curtain over the protesters. The second chopper dropped another, and the first, another. The protesters were scattering in every direction.

"It's RAIN. Those fuckers," Morgan said. Tzaro recognized the crowd control agent.

"Only police can—"

"It's corporate security. They've got it…Mesmark."

They scrambled to their feet.

Tzaro checked desperately for Therica. She had vanished from the clearing. No movement in the trees. He felt Morgan clutch his arm.

One of the helicopters was leaving the crowd at the far end, banking toward their end of the park. His first thought was back to the woods for cover. Therica's perimeter was too far—the chopper would cut them off.

"You should go now."

The voice from behind startled him. It was urgent but assured.

"Wilson."

"Both of you, especially her."

Green spray was dropping from the chopper between them and the clearing.

Wilson began jogging back to the closest woods, and Tzaro and Morgan broke after him. They crashed into the underbrush and then they were in the trees. Wilson kept on until they reached the shadows under a heavy canopy. They all bent over, hands on knees, panting. Sirens were arriving from the direction of the clearing.

"You were being followed," Wilson said, deep eyes fixed on Morgan. "A guy was getting close to you when Tzaro found you. I think he had a Trakker."

Tzaro envisioned the stalker focused on his phone with a morph-recog app, locked on to Morgan's face and form.

She hung her head, looked back up, face glistening with sweat. From a hardness in her look, Tzaro guessed it wasn't the first time.

"We have to catch up," she said. "She's probably heading for the house."

"Not so sure." Her apartment, the lab, anywhere, Tzaro was thinking, the image of her wild-eyed still white-hot.

"Let's start there; we're losing time." Morgan was standing, ready and more.

The sirens were louder. Police were close, in the park.

He got her, completely. But he had more information. He couldn't tell how or why, but he knew he had the key to what possessed Therica. And he was becoming chillingly aware her sudden mania was not unique. He felt his pants pocket to confirm the disc of bubble memory the thickness of an old nickel. He knew the source already, but now it meant more. It had a sudden velocity, and weight, and a range he couldn't gauge. He knew what he knew, but it made it no easier. His assistant of the last ten months was in his heart, much more than a lab partner. A chopper whacked by overhead, deafening above the trees, and it felt to him like the thrashing in his insides.

"I need to get to the city," he said to Wilson. "The ferry will be jammed."

"What are you..." Morgan started, clearly appalled.

"Listen, we can help her, but not here. There's a reason she's like this. And not just Therica, there are others. Trust me."

"Where do you need to go?" Wilson asked.

"The U, there's a professor—"

"We can use my boat. We should go now." Wilson rose to his full height.

Tzaro had been unsure, but that Wilson had a boat struck him as a sign, if he could believe in signs.

"You're going to freaking leave her?" Morgan was cold. "Should I be surprised." She started back toward the clearing.

"Hey, queen of the revolution, you have no clue."

She stopped.

"You don't know what I'm about, or what happened to her, or what's going on here." He was fighting for Therica, he knew, but he was feeling nearly as possessed, going on something totally irrational, but true. "All of that I can understand and excuse. But if you think we have another option and I'm not taking it, you're deluding yourself for your own reasons."

Morgan was staring at him, breathing hard, fists clenched. Out of a rumble like a storm, the whacking was closing in, thundering down.

"Behind you," Wilson shouted.

Between Morgan and the clearing, green mist was dropping, fogging the firs and cedars.

And then it was on her.

Tzaro bolted forward, grabbed her hand.

"Come on!" Wilson hopped a log and bounded easily into the deeper forest.

Tzaro's eyes met Morgan's. Their hands were tight.

Then they were trying to keep up with Wilson, who was nimbly dodging the broken ivy-wrapped trees and moss-green stumps in the shadows, as though everywhere he ran was Indian land.

CHAPTER 7   PROFESSOR CAL

Wilson kept his boat in an aluminum boathouse at the bottom of his yard that faced the flat water east of Orcas. As they watched on his dock, he slid the door open. The gray fiberglass hull looked sleek as a shark poised to drop the four feet into the light waves that slapped against the dock posts and echoed.

After a mile plus of hiking through forest, they had picked up a trail and then a dirt road that led to Wilson's land on the water. Soon after they started, Tzaro realized he had nothing, only his clothes, the memory disc in his pocket, and his wallet. No tools. No phone.

Wilson pressed the button inside the door and the boat began to descend. Morgan looked away over the water then glanced back at the woods, as though Therica would come out waving. Tzaro saw a muscle working in her jaw.

"Look, I'm sorry to ask," he said, "but do you have a phone?"

She looked at him as though inspecting an insect.

"I left mine in my car. I know how this probably sounds, but I don't use it that much. I have to contact someone to meet us."

She let the stare linger for a noticeable breath then swung her backpack off onto the dock.

Nervously, Tzaro fished in his wallet behind the cards. Between folded notes, he found the worn business card where he kept old phone numbers. He scanned the names and numbers printed small and rotated in the margins. Then he was breathing easy: Prof. Carmody, and his mobile number.

Morgan handed over her ancient Galaxy.

"Dude!" Tzaro enthused. "Same era! I have an iPhone 6, a little bent. At least I can still make calls."

"They're metal," she said, looser.

He nodded. Titanium, he was thinking, but no problem.

He patted Wilson's shoulder as the boat hit bottom. "Just give me a sec."

Prof. Carmody. That was a while ago. Tzaro knew when he wrote it, following his commencement, Masters in Geology, University of Washington. He had been a star student in those days, two decades ago, especially in Calvin Carmody's Archaeology. Carmody sponsored his thesis, on intraplate quakes and paleoseismology in the New Madrid seismic zone, third millennium B.C. At the commencement reception, Carmody had given his number, which Tzaro recorded on his first Caltech business card. Carmody's recommendation sealed his application. Professor Carmody taught archaeology, but even then his specialty was ancient languages. That was why Tzaro was calling. And he didn't call him "Professor Carmody" anymore. He had dined in the Carmody's home with Lauren before they were married, and he had met the professor again a year earlier in his current life, soon after leaving Pasadena. If asked his reasons for lobbying as hard as he had for his position on Orcas, career building would not be one. If the first was distance and solitude, the second could easily have been Calvin Carmody.

"Cal, it's Tzaro Janssen. How are you?" He looked out over the water, envisioning Cal in his office on campus. His digital voice, its natural energy only slightly diminished, sounded pleased. Once again, his face came into clear focus.

"Well, thanks. I have a favor to ask. Could we possibly meet in your office? Right, today.

"I need your help to understand some glyphs, pictographs. It's a matter of some urgency. I think it may—yes, that's great. Understand. Three is perfect. Thank you. See you then."

Wilson had the boat down. With Morgan in the middle, he was hand-walking it to the end of the dock. Tzaro swung his leg over the rail, took Wilson's hand, and touched down in the fiberglass hull. He took the seat in front of Morgan's, a rotating chair with a chrome rod holder cup between his legs.

Wilson started the 150-horse Mercury outboard, and the Boston Whaler Montauk bucked and leveled. They struck out over Rosario Strait, slapping down the waves, spraying white wings on both sides of the bow.

"This is a safe slip." Wilson pitched the bow line around a pole on the dock. "Earl will keep his eye on it. He's an elder who takes care of everything here at the center. That's Daybreak Star."

They disembarked in Discovery Park. The Daybreak Star Center sat at the top of the hill, a timber and glass building adorned with native art, a totem pole and a longboat on the front grounds. Tzaro had never been in the park, but he knew it was on the north side of the city.

"How far is UW?" he asked as they started up the hill.

"That way," Wilson said, striding in front of him.

"My question was, how far?"

"Hour, maybe more."

Tzaro focused on the gravel path, imagining it was more like *maybe more*. Don't ask, he reminded himself, if you don't want to hear the answer.

Past a parking lot, they reached a two-lane asphalt road. "I don't want to hear it," Morgan said. "All right? Over there." She pointed to the outside of the shoulder where the men were clearly being directed to stand. Then she dropped her pack beside her foot, rolled up her commando pants legs, put her left fist on her hip, and stuck out her right thumb.

"Okay, you can stay," Tzaro told her on the sidewalk on Forty-fifth Street at the north end of the University of Washington campus.

The Hyundai Cadre all-terrain rolled away. The driver was a soldier from Joint Base Lewis-McChord who had stopped with high hopes, but when he saw the two guys, he had already committed and couldn't refuse to take them all.

Wilson tossed a laugh into the air.

"You're welcome," Morgan said, deadpan, then bent over to roll down her pants legs.

"It's close," Tzaro said, and they started up the hill.

The brick quadrangle of Red Square held the heat of the August afternoon. It was deserted except for a couple in the shade of a distant column and a lone Asian girl biking away toward the dorms.

"Wow," Morgan said. Suitably awed, Tzaro thought. "Is this open?"

They had reached the steps of the Suzzallo Library. The towering Gothic facade was adorned with sculpted figures on buttresses and enormous shields bearing university crests. In each of the three entrance portals stood columns topped with statues against sculpted branches that appeared to sprout from the stone. Tzaro and the others entered through the center portal as though into a cathedral, and he pulled the heavy door.

The familiar smell greeted him, cool stone. One male student exited without eye contact as they entered, and they were alone in the soaring foyer.

"This way." He bore right, onto a grand staircase, broad stone steps worn by thousands of students, stained glass high in the casement walls.

At the top of the stairs he entered a hall, tile floor, vaulted ceiling of steel buttresses, antique glass world globes suspended, glowing from within. Wilson and Morgan followed, silent, wide-eyed. For Tzaro, his former life came flooding back—thesis meetings in Carmody's garret office, life before marriage. He flashed on Sunday. Wherever he was, he needed to call Derek.

Of the three office doors at the end of the hall, Tzaro stopped at the last: *Dr. Calvin Carmody, Ancient Languages.* He knocked twice. The door opened as though the professor had been waiting with his hand on the knob.

"Tzaro, so good to see you." He bear-hugged his guest and pounded his back. Carmody was short and solid with a shaved head and wireframe glasses. Although probably in his late sixties, he seemed younger with movements quick and compact like a wrestler's. "Please, come in. Your friends?"'

They exchanged pleasantries and the three settled in chairs. Morgan looked diminutive in the leather wing chair where Tzaro had sat during his thesis meetings. Floor-to-ceiling bookcases adorned the back wall. On several of the shelves, and on the chest beside leaded windows, light stone tablets, each speckled with glyphs, stood in black frames. Carmody leaned back against the front of his massive desk with slate top, facing them, two monitors behind him.

"To what do I owe this honor?" He was smiling, but he had settled his energetic greeting into sudden quiet and focused intently on Tzaro. It was Cal's listening mode and it felt familiar. "You mentioned some writing."

"It may be writing, but pre-alphabetic. Pictographic. I have screen grabs, thirty-two per second from Wundrus, the social media site."

Carmody's eyebrows rose in recognition.

"There's an image, circular, a kind of mandala; the characters are in the center. The image occurs every second for a sixteenth of a second. It's perfectly regular, nonrandom. At that frequency it's subliminal. And I think it's for a purpose. It's...affecting people. My lab assistant is one."

Morgan may have been skeptical, but she was listening intently too.

"And I think," Tzaro went on, "there are others. Maybe many others."

"I take it you have the captures? Let's have a look."

Carmody rounded his desk and seemed to hop into his chair. Tzaro produced the disc and Wilson and Morgan joined him behind the professor's chair. In a few moments Carmody had the first of the captures, frame image twenty-eight, displayed on his right monitor.

"Yes, you're right, excellent," he said. "A mandala."

The image filling the screen was circular—a circle with an inscribed square, and at the center, the two shapes repeated. Silver and red seemed to float over a background of deep green.

"The mandala is primarily a Buddhist symbol, first mentioned in the Rig Veda. Sanskrit origin. This one is purely geometric—no Buddhist symbology. It's used as a meditation aid—to free the subconscious, and possibly induce a trancelike state."

Yes, Tzaro thought but didn't interrupt.

"Now we see there are four gates to the outer circle instead of three. We in the West would expect a triumvirate, but here the outer circle is not the most significant. We see here in the heart circle..."

Carmody paused, studying.

"Would you please bring me the book on the second shelf there, the one with a white jacket..." He was talking to Morgan who was closest, pointing to the center bookcase.

"*Ideographic Scripts*," she read the spine.

"Yes, that's it."

Morgan delivered the ponderous volume, coffee-table-size, edges of the pages marbled with colored inks. Carmody took it with both hands. He turned to the second monitor and depressed the audio button in the lower right corner.

"East Asia pictogram," he said. A list of links opened with headings: China, Japan, Korea. He flipped open the book, thumbed the pages.

"In the heart circle," he picked up, "yes, Tzaro, you are quite correct. It's a pictographic syntax."

Carmody read a passage to himself then clicked on one of the links. Morgan, Wilson, and Tzaro were wax figures, hanging on his next word.

"But it is not an ancient language."

"I thought Sumerian, maybe Akkadian." Tzaro was sinking inside. Possibly Carmody couldn't help him.

"Those, except for the earliest examples, were cuneiform, not truly pictographic."

Carmody swiped through screens, then compared one to the open book.

"No, not ancient at all," he confirmed. "This is Dongba, a script of the Naxi culture of China. It was developed in the seventh century, Tang Dynasty. It's the only pictographic writing in the world that's maintained to this day."

"Can you—"

"Decode it? Well, let me see, there are over a thousand symbols. If you can amuse yourselves for a bit. The campus café is closed, but you know there are several on the Ave."

"Great, Cal, thanks so much."

"Don't thank me yet. My only guarantee is, no guarantees." Carmody was already smooth head down, thumbing through pages.

"We'll stay close." Tzaro led the others into the hall.

"Why don't you two get something on University Avenue. It's a block below where we got out. I'll hang here. Get me any kind of coffee and a sandwich, okay?" He handed Wilson two twenties, one of the few denominations that remained. "That's for gas, too," he said. "No change."

"You're the boss," Wilson said and turned to go, but Morgan lingered.

"I hope your professor has a revelation," she said, "but I can't see where this is going. You're saying people hitting sites like Wundrus are getting hypnotized by a subliminal image and a bunch of characters nobody can read but a sect of Chinese who've never heard of social media. While Therica—"

"Look, let this play out, all right? If it's nothing we'll cruise back and get Orcas police."

Morgan stared at him like a stiff-lipped emoji. She and Wilson headed down the hall, and then he heard them on the stairs.

Tzaro looked out a leaded window over the campus, a view he had seen many times in his previous lifetime. In a moment he was seeing Therica as she had been in the clearing, and in the woods, raking his arm like a trapped animal and breaking away. He could be wrong, but he didn't think so. He knew her. And if the image was compelling her in some way... San Diego flashed by, and Bethesda. Pasadena and Derek. He was feeling suddenly cold, as though he had witnessed an accident. He started to hope he was wrong. Outside one of the other offices he saw a chair, and he sat down to wait.

He went to familiar territory. And it was safe because he had no phone, and Morgan's was well out of range.

Six-seven-eight, eight-seven-four, twenty-three thirty.

She had sent the number to all her friends years ago when she moved to Atlanta. He carried it in his wallet, but he had memorized it too, in case he ever got the nerve to call, and was in possession of the means.

This recall was an exercise only, a memory check. Plus, he found it soothing. He repeated her number silently, his mantra, with no reason to believe it still worked.

When he heard his name called, the rotating doorknob had already snapped him awake. He was surprised to have nodded off.

"Yes," Carmody said, "we have something." He hustled back into the office and Tzaro followed.

"The Dongba pictographic alphabet, though a quite extensive set of logograms, is not fully representative of the Naxi language. It can be supplemented with a syllabic script... I'll wait for your friends."

Morgan and Wilson reappeared in the office door.

"Glad you made it," Tzaro said. His coffee cup and sandwich went on the desk and they all gathered behind Carmody's chair. Opposite frame twenty-eight on his right monitor, his left was littered with small stick figures.

"As I was saying, these symbols can be supplemented with a syllabic alphabet, but I think we have enough here. The characters are read, or more accurately, interpreted, as an ideogrammatic cluster, a kind of mosaic." He pointed to the center of the mandala.

"These two, taken together..." He pointed to two symbols on the other monitor, side-by-side. "Represent faith, or belief.

"This one is more controversial, with two distinct connotations. The first is 'chief' or 'ruler'. This was one of the original couple of hundred characters, and that was the original meaning. Since the turn of the first millennium..." He pointed to a translation in the book. "The common connotation has been the concept of selfhood—ego or self.

"Of these final symbols, the first is quite obvious, the generic everyman. Beneath him is this character." He swiped down two screens and pointed to an exact replica. "A field, plain, or grassland."

"It's like a word puzzle," Morgan said.

"Faith, ruler-self, man-field," Tzaro tried to cobble the terms.

"Faith, or trust," Carmody said, as though adding a clue.

"Faith-trust, self, man-field," Morgan tested.

"Have faith in yourself…" Tzaro tried again.

"The man in the field," Wilson said suddenly, "he's standing alone."

"Exactly!" Carmody nearly shouted.

"Faith, self, alone," Morgan said, and they were quiet then as the message was coming clearer, revealing itself.

Carmody nodded, then summarized: "Trust yourself only."

CHAPTER 8   SVETLA

They turned the phrase in their heads. Morgan broke the silence.

"This is it? How can you think this made Therica—"

"She was seeing this for a sixteenth of a second every second she was on Wundrus." Tzaro locked onto her eyes, skeptical, gray. "It's subliminal messaging, going back to TV advertising before it was regulated. 'Trust yourself only'—that's where she is now, isn't it? And think of the number of people seeing it, hooked—in a mandala. As Cal said, it's used to induce trance. Wundrus has what, three billion users? And that's not including Ping and Uptake. I haven't checked those, but I'd be surprised—"

"If they were hacked, it would be all over, everywhere," she countered.

"Cal, could you search?"

Carmody tried all the keywords.

"I see only pieces on hacking Wundrus for personal data, in 2021."

"Okay, I get the mandala," Morgan went on, "but what is it without the message? How are people supposed to get it? It's a language nobody reads but a micro-population of Chinese, am I right?" She directed it at Carmody.

"That's certainly true, for the most part. Except for a small band of academics."

"Not a problem," Wilson said. "We don't have to read to understand."

"Exactly," Tzaro said, shooting him with his index finger. "These pictographs, images, are operating on a subconscious level. They're being perceived outside a rational framework that depends on conscious decoding. There's nothing blocking our ability to perceive them directly, below the level of consciousness. They do look like what they represent. Yes, we were challenged to map them to their exact analogs in English. But I felt this, and I bet you did—as Cal suggested the optional interpretations of each character... they fit."

"We didn't know the words," Wilson said, "but we knew the meaning."

Morgan was pacing.

"All right, all right. I hear you about the picture language. But your subliminal message thing, it's way overrated. Believe it or don't, I was a Psych major once, when Therica was Geology. I remember at least in those days, subliminal messaging didn't make people act in ways they didn't intend to already."

"That's quite right," Carmody chimed in with enthusiasm. "But priming studies have shown those who were inclined to act were significantly influenced to act. Tipped, as it were."

Doubt pinched a wrinkle between her eyebrows.

"And I'm talking about exposure for a sixteenth of a second," Tzaro went on, "every second that people are viewing Wundrus. If it's the big three sites, then over four billion people. Around the world. And the longer they're online, the more exposure—"

"Sorry, but I think you're way off here," Morgan said. "This is like... not real. I'm going back." She looked at Wilson. "If you could take me, super, I'll pay the gas. If not..." She went for her backpack on the chair.

Tzaro stepped between her and the door.

"Okay, look. I'll get this to the authorities and they can make the call. Okay? I think you could be really helpful here. To Therica. Everybody."

"Authorities?"

"FBI."

"Oh yeah, you see what you get there." Morgan was shaking her head but she put the backpack down.

"Thank you," he said. "Thank you."

"Where to, boss?" Wilson said.

Carmody had found the address of the FBI field office.

"Eleven-ten Third Avenue," he said, grinning like a kid.

"Sparky!" Wilson said. "You are quick, man. Sparky-quick. Oh yes."

"It's Saturday," Tzaro said. "I should call. Does it give a number?"

"They said somebody could talk to me today, but the guy I really need is out of state, coming in tonight. He's a senior special agent, experience in cyberterrorism. I have an appointment tomorrow at eleven."

Morgan looked tight as a spring. She paced two steps to the bookcase, then back.

"A Sunday? Tomorrow could be as good as a year," she said.

"And it could also crack this."

She took the chair with her backpack, looking nothing like convinced.

Tzaro caught a view out of Carmody's side window, over Red Square. Empty.

"Where to now?" Wilson repeated.

"We can get a room," Tzaro said. "Or rooms," he corrected. "On me."

"If I may," Carmody said, "you'd be most welcome to stay with me. Tipi is speaking at a conference—ornithology, you know."

"Cal, I've imposed enough already."

"Nonsense, you'll save an old man from a lonely evening. I insist."

Tzaro recalled the capacious old house in Wallingford with a distant view of Lake Union.

"Outrageously nice of you."

Carmody was already shutting down, then he bounded out of the office first, waiting for them so he could lock up.

They left the Suzzallo and descended the hill to the edge of campus. Tzaro saw only two students crossing the grounds alone in the heat of afternoon. He knew it was walking distance to the house, although a bit of a hike. Carmody chose that moment to explain about their destination.

"It's only three blocks, right one and up two, a block from Twelfth. Faculty housing, part of the new collaboration policy, you know. Oh yes, all of us, tenured and not. We must model a community of learners, an Athens of the Northwest."

"The school ordered you out of your house?" Tzaro was shocked, even though he knew colleges that still paid salaries for old-style classroom instructors could require whatever they pleased.

"Ordered? Oh no, not at all. We have the option to become assistant professors, basically part-time contractors. It's not so bad. We're renting the house—two couples, all aerospace engineers. It's like a Boeing commune."

"Cal, listen, we can't do this. You don't have room—"

"It's no problem, believe me. With Tipi on the road, it's two full bedrooms. Plus, we have an air mattress—"

Tzaro remembered only rounding a blind corner with a tall building close to the sidewalk. He felt the impact on his right arm, a glancing blow. She was a dashing blur and a whisk of dark hair. Morgan was down behind him, sprawled on the sidewalk, the young woman who had collided with her down beside her, struggling to sit up.

"Bitch!" came from the direction she had been fleeing.

"He's going to kill me!" She was on one knee, a slight twenty-something with huge dark eyes.

Tzaro turned to her pursuer, half a block out and closing hard. Medium height but burly, shaved head and goatee, in a nice shirt, plum-colored, silky sheen.

It had been Tzaro and Carmody in front, Morgan and Wilson behind, but now Tzaro sensed Wilson beside him, on the street side of the walk.

The guy slowed but didn't stop.

"Hang on!" Tzaro shouted at him, but he was already on them like a high school fullback.

Tzaro got an arm up to absorb the impact, but there was none, only a whiff of too-sweet cologne.

Wilson hooked the pursuer's arm and used his own momentum to spin him off the sidewalk and into the street. The guy stumbled and went down then scrambled up fuming, apparently thinking of taking another run, but Wilson and Tzaro were shoulder-to-shoulder between him and the girl.

"Take it! Here, take it!" The woman joined them and pitched something into the street—a wallet, cards spilling onto the asphalt.

"Goddamn you, Julia! Bitch!" He scrambled around, picking up the pieces.

"Take it! I don't want your fucking wallet! Fucker!"

"One charge, Julia, that's all I need. One charge and I'll have your ass! You heard me!"

He slunk off in the direction he had come, shaking his shiny head and swearing.

Julia went to Morgan, helped her up.

"I'm so sorry. Are you all right? He is crazy asshole American. Saudi-American asshole." Her accent sounded Russian or Slavic. She patted Morgan's arms as though dusting them off.

"He thought I was using his credit card, like what do you say, a thief of identity. He is paranoid. I'm lucky I never moved in, which is what he wanted." Morgan was bending her knee.

"Did I hurt you? We really clunked there. We hit knees. You know that song 'Crash into Me'?" Morgan couldn't keep from laughing. Her crash-mate laughed too.

"I don't want his freaking credit cards. But he had all my numbers in his wallet—phone, banking. Not anymore. I have it." She pulled a folded sheet of notebook paper from the pocket of her tight jeans then crammed it back in.

"That's what that was about." She made the final announcement like testimony to a jury.

Around arresting dark eyes, her face seemed aerodynamically contoured, an illusion created by her hair, which was pulled tightly into a ponytail, the dark whip of hair that had caught Tzaro's eye when she dashed past him. From the back of her head to the front, a little left of center, ran a two-inch stripe of blue. On her slender body all was sleek and form-fitting, a deep purple tank top and light jeans that ended above her knees. Despite her slight form, she was voluptuous on top. Tzaro realized he could be wrong, but he imagined Morgan looked interested.

"And I want to thank you for helping me." She turned to Tzaro and Wilson. "You are *muzhestven chovek*, as they say in my country. Most macho."

"And is your country perhaps Turkey, or Macedonia?" Carmody asked.

"Between the two. I am Bulgarian."

"And your name is Julia?" Tzaro asked.

"No, I was Julia to him only. For whatsoever he knows. My name is Svetla. That's my real name, to people I trust."

As they introduced themselves, Tzaro wondered if she had other names. She seemed comfortable switching them.

"Are you going somewhere?" she asked.

"Actually, we are going to—" Carmody started.

"Get a place to stay tonight," Tzaro cut in. "We all have something to do in the morning."

"You need a place. Good, okay," she said forthrightly. "I am happy to do this. You saved my butt, they say. You can stay at my accommodation. Seven hundred square meters, including share bath, full kitchen. Twenty-five per night. All of you, I don't care. I have air mattresses."

Tzaro checked the others, who were thumbs up. Carmody insisted on going along, suggesting, sensibly, that they might need his help again.

"Where?" Tzaro asked their new acquaintance.

"Come on," Svetla said. "I am Guber driver."

CHAPTER 9   GEORGETOWN NIGHT

Svetla's car was big enough for all of them—Tzaro, Wilson, and Carmody in back, Morgan in front on the passenger side. Wilson had it pegged: Mercury Grand Marquis. The last one he saw, he was a kid on the reservation. It was on blocks by a trailer, a big bad V-8 between transmissions.

They descended on I-5 from the U District, crossing the bridge over a glittering Lake Union. Boats tracked its length, and a float plane was lifting, heading north. The Space Needle slid by on their right, and they stayed on the highway as it skirted the city center. Soon they were on the south side. Svetla angled off at an exit, and a block from the ramp they saw a neighborhood sign: Georgetown.

It was a zone of industrial buildings spotted with gentrification and dusted with outré—trendy bars, hair salons, tech shops, and boutiques. Tzaro only wanted quick access to downtown Seattle, and Georgetown had to be. He had counted only two exits after they passed the core. Svetla pulled up outside a brick monolith.

"Cool car," he said as they climbed out. "It's kind of a classic."

"I know." She was on the front steps in two strides, producing her keys, old-style, no fob. "I get a lot of fares because of it. A guy I knew wanted to get rid of it. He made it look like a present. It is top page on Guber site. They like to feature their human drivers, like they're your friendly company." She turned the second key and they were in. Down a short hall to the left of the stone staircase was another door, and Svetla opened a final lock.

"Wow, nice," Morgan said.

Tzaro was inclined to agree. Steel I-beams traversed the ceiling the full length of the building. Hardwood flooring, shellacked but wheel-rutted, ran to a shadowy vanishing point. In the long brick wall on the left, two industrial fans hummed in window casements, and the other tall windows, painted over white, emitted a creamy light. Overhead, draped from the beams, strands of Christmas lights twinkled holiday colors.

"Your rooms..." Svetla led them down the floor toward the opposite wall.

"The bathroom, with shower." She pointed to the first of a series of Sheetrock enclosures, doors hung with bead or bamboo curtains.

"My place is here," she indicated the next door, "and yours—"

From a point unseen around one of the far baffles, a figure came rolling toward them on a skateboard, rumbling over the hardwood. A young woman, dark hair under a Dodgers cap—Philippine, Tzaro guessed—in a white body stocking, orange flames and sequins on her legs. She raised a hand as she cruised by, and Svetla waved back. A second behind her, a black man in Captain America tights rolled a loop over the floor and followed the woman with a toodle-loo wave.

"Mara and Marco are in Cirque du Soleil. You can have these three. I will bring mattresses."

They checked their accommodations behind the bead curtains. Each room was the size of an ample bedroom with assorted furnishings. A wooden cable spool on end was the standard table. Chairs varied from overstuffed and collapsed to various restaurant and white plastic models. Tzaro guessed the fruit crates served for drawers.

Svetla returned with both arms full of air mattresses, dropped them on the floor, and went to work with a foot pump.

"Please," Carmody said after the first was full. "I have one of these myself." He manned the pump with an eager smile and his foot pistoned up and down.

"What kind of factory?" Wilson asked.

"Beer," she said. "Brewery. This floor is where they stored kegs."

"A great loft space," Tzaro said. "How did you find it?"

"I know the owner. He wanted someone else to rent. He makes beer too but not here. It is a carved beer business."

"Craft beer?"

"Yes, *craft*."

Carmody presented a firm mattress to Morgan and she tried it out.

"It is like the mattresses," Svetla went on. "That was another beer guy, but pizza and beer, mainly pizza. A lot of Bulgarians are in the pizza business. It didn't work out and he was trying to sell these on I-Buy. He wanted me to marry him, but I took these off his hands instead. A better decision. He is back in Bulgaria now."

No problem making male friends, Tzaro was getting the picture, some more long-lived than others.

Morgan took the first room, and Tzaro and Wilson doubled up in the middle, giving the professor his own room on the end.

"Have you tried her?" Tzaro asked Morgan. He guessed she had only been waiting until they were out of the car to phone Therica again.

"Just did."

"Sorry to ask you again. I need to call in."

"Whenever," she said and turned over her phone.

"Jerry. Tzaro.

"Right, no, we haven't gone in since this morning. There's an issue with Therica... Not sure, an emotional crisis of some kind. I'm in the city with somebody I think can help.

"No, I don't know where she is right now. Look, I need a big favor. Can you take it remotely for a couple of days? Save any action up here for me—I'll handle it when I get in.

"I'm not sure when yet, a couple of days. I'll be in by Wednesday, Thursday latest." Long pause. He could hear Jerry's pain. They were taking a chance with the lab empty. "Absolutely, I'll let you know if there's an issue.

"Thanks, man. I owe you."

Tzaro paid Svetla for their night's lodging and ordered pizzas for all. They planned to be at the FBI office early. Before they parted for the night, Morgan tried Therica's phone again. After the rings they could all hear her voice mail.

"Should you notify the police on the island?" Carmody put it to him as a question, rhetorically obvious.

"We'll have to in the morning, but I want them to have all the information, including anything the FBI can tell us. Orcas police alone could do more harm than good. If I'm right, this is out of their league."

Tzaro showered last in the Sheetrock surround. On his back on an air mattress across from Wilson whose feet overhung his mattress but who was out nevertheless, he tried to weigh the odds of being right. And if he was right, what it could possibly mean. He had taken the third beer to bed and chugged it until he could focus on the morning and what he would do then, and then the focus blurred.

At an indeterminate time he woke to a rumble like a train through the loft, but a small one, casters on wood. Mara and

Marco, he realized, rolling back home. He turned over but it was useless. The revenge of the beer. He would have to walk the hardwood.

Before the bathroom, half-asleep and trying to preserve the half, he passed Svetla's bamboo curtains. He heard her voice, a little above a whisper.

"I fucking hate myself, 'cause I dropped out. My father is a school principal in my town. I was going to be a teacher. Great fucking teacher. I've done some loser things, shoplifting and more than that. I've got a record. Maybe I've got a diagnosis, an American diagnosis—fucked up." She laughed and whimpered.

"Hey, my parents." It was Morgan's voice. Tzaro stood in his underwear in the breeze of the fan that was almost cool and he needed to, he knew, but he could not tear himself away. "They always thought I would be hitched by now and have my own house. Sometimes—okay, a lot of the time now—that doesn't seem so bad. The house anyway," she laughed quietly.

Then Tzaro heard no talk, but not silence either—sounds of comforting, and pleasure. He felt his way through the curtain next door and sat to pee as quietly as he could.

On his back again in the closeness of the August night, Wilson snoring into the wall, he stared up into an aurora of Christmas lights and, thinking of Morgan and Svetla, and considering the vast capacities of the human heart, said why not. Soon he was on his own journey of the heart, in Atlanta, under a webwork of stars.

CHAPTER 10   THANKS FOR YOUR INPUT

"Are you aware of any other instances of this imagery? On other social sites, for example?" FBI Special Agent Patel was studying his screen and the frames from Tzaro's bubble memory.

"No, I haven't sampled the others. That should be done right away. I'm sure you have—"

"Yes, we do have high-frequency sampling capability." Patel spoke quietly and with precision, and his white shirt was crisp even on a Sunday. Tzaro placed him mid-to-late forties. At least the expert on cyberterrorism had the age potential for experience. Assistant Special Agent Liu looked early thirties. He had brought in extra chairs for Morgan, Wilson, and Carmody. By light rail they had arrived at the field office early. Only Svetla had remained in the loft.

"And you believe viewing this subliminal image has acted as a kind of psychological trigger on Ms. Lundy." A printout of Therica's lab profile lay on Patel's desk, together with basic background FBI data. As expected, Liu had immediately filed a missing person's report with Orcas police.

"Yes! Yes, and on many others. You've heard, they're all over the news ... San Diego, and that girl in Bethesda. The others... Europe... somewhere in Germany. No doubt others as we speak."

Patel stared at Tzaro, wolf eyes, gray-blue.

"First, I want to assure you, as soon as Orcas police locate Ms. Lundy, they'll notify you. They have the contact phone you gave us. We have requested on your behalf, and police departments... cooperate."

Tzaro wanted to have a feeling that something masterful was going to happen, but he didn't.

"That's great," he said. "Thank you."

"And I'd like to thank *you* for bringing this to our attention. Citizen participation is key to everything we do, and often, for reasons we all understand, citizens are unwilling to do what you did, come forward and make it a team effort."

Liu nodded like a discreet bobblehead.

"Now, regarding those other cases. As I'm sure you can appreciate," Patel regarded his full audience, "we treat every case as what it is—unique. Naturally, we also look for commonalities. If we can identify a common thread, that helps us. All law enforcement, if we can see—"

"Point taken," Morgan cut in. "Connections are good."

Patel and Liu stiffened.

Morgan went wide-eyed, as in *go on.*

"Regardless of the similarities that media dwell on for their purposes, these cases don't all have a common source. However," Patel paused, "some of them do share a common thread.

"In relation to several of the cases in Europe, the World Health Organization has identified a factor with a high level of confidence. I'll show you something now that hasn't been released to the public." He rotated his screen. "This page on the WHO site is being reviewed. As soon as it's approved it will go live."

Tzaro and the others scanned.

"Ergot?" he said.

"As you see, the effects of this fungus, which lives in food grains—rye, wheat—were documented over two thousand years ago. Dissociative reactions, psychotic episodes, lethal violence. The essential components are related to LSD. Some grain crops in the Rhône Valley seem to have tested positive."

"Grain poisoning? All of these incidents?"

"The cases are under investigation," Liu continued, nodding, echoing his boss. "Any correlations will be tracked—"

"But what about the cases here? We aren't eating German wheat—"

"The Center for Disease Control in Atlanta monitors a range of bio-factors." Patel took it back. "It appears *toxoplasma gondii* may play a role."

"Cat craziness," Morgan translated. "You know, the virus that infects cat lovers, makes them wacko."

"An extraordinarily virulent strain, a powerful mutation. The CDC's hypothesis is just that, theoretical at this point. What we have here is something of a war of research camps." Patel grinned stiffly.

"But regardless of the winner, any common factors are a matter of biological pathogens, not cyberterrorism. As we know, cyber attacks pose a threat to entire democratic governments, and we have sensitive tools of detection and multilevel arrays of defenses against them. We have no data to indicate a relation between your images and cyber aggression. The kind of mind control we've been discussing simply isn't in their playbook. We do have an idea of what you've discovered, though."

Patel clearly favored the pregnant pause. Liu looked as spellbound as the rest of them.

"You're a seismologist, Mr. Janssen. I'm guessing you've encountered programmers in your line of work? Perhaps you've noticed—if we can generalize a bit—they tend to be something of a special breed. Just as it's traditional for painters to sign their works, programmers sometimes include a kind of signature in theirs, sometimes embedded in the source code—you should see some of those—and sometimes hidden in plain sight. What we have here is an instance of a programmer marking his or her creation with a personal stamp, a kind of tag.

"I think if you pursue your research, you'll find this is specific to this website, an 'inside job' by a lone programmer or perhaps a small team. I'm sure the owners of this site would be grateful to know what you've discovered. They might even give you an ad-free account. I hear some are doing that now." He nearly chuckled.

"What we'd like to do, though, is keep a copy of your image and run it against our database of these markers. If there's no match, we'll add it. Sometimes they're useful in confirming the source of hacks, usually denial of service by a botnet, that sort of thing." Patel's eyebrows lifted. They said, *your move.*

CHAPTER 11   G-MEN

"Is that maybe what we call a supercilious prick?" Morgan fumed as soon as they were in the hall.

"But he knows his business, supposedly." Tzaro said. "May I again…"

Morgan handed over her phone.

As they left the building and headed down the hill toward the water, he pulled up the number of the main office in D.C. Enunciating clearly, he spoke to the bot: "cyberterrorism." The voice asked for his ZIP Code. He was being transferred, and a familiar recording answered, the Seattle field office. He hung up.

He tried Seattle police, claiming he had information about a missing person's case. On the second transfer he spoke to a young detective who was unable to locate any record in the system of a missing person named Lundy. For his concerns regarding cyberterrorism, she told Tzaro to contact the Seattle office of the FBI and volunteered the number.

"It's a conspiracy of idiots." Tzaro was trying to envision his next move and coming up empty. They had reached Pike Place Market and a park on the end with a totem pole in the center of a knoll and a sparkling view over Elliott Bay. It would have been glorious on any other pellucid August Sunday.

"The ergot hypothesis seems far-fetched, I agree." Carmody was straining a sympathy muscle.

"Patel was so sure it was a nerd prank—a graffiti tag," Tzaro went on. "Would your average programmer sign his code in Dongba?"

"He's a prick, all right?" Morgan explained. Tzaro had a bad feeling about what was coming next.

"They have your frames. They have to check it out. 'The citizen comes forward.' Dickhead said it himself. They have a lot of firepower to work with. Believe me, anybody with a record for anything knows that. Maybe you've done all you can."

She looked out over the bay. He handed her phone back.

"What are you going to do?" Carmody asked.

Tzaro took a breath. He half-shook his head.

Through the meeting and after, all the way down the hill to the end of the market, its corner pinned by the Haida totem pole, Wilson had been quiet.

"You and the G-men," he said. "Remember G-men? I saw that in a comic book when I was a kid. It was my grandmother's. She had a collection of comic books on the reservation, most of them from when she was a girl in Montana. The G-men, the FBI. You and the G-men have something in common, my friend. They don't know either." Wilson reported it as a fact. It reminded Tzaro of his mechanical certainties when he worked on the Tesla. And of his telling Morgan she was being followed in the park.

"The Chinese," he said. "He tried to show nothing, but he was showing a lot. They don't know what it is. They know the problem—it's why they met with you today. But they don't believe you. They don't believe the science guys either—"

"But they can't admit that?" Morgan cut in. "They need a story, until they can figure it out."

"Or until somebody can show them," Wilson completed the thought.

"So they won't help you. Why am I not surprised?" Svetla crunched a carrot stick. They were sitting around the table in the loft, and she had just heard all of the story that Morgan hadn't already told her.

"But I say, you have the woman who's gone crazy and missing. You have stories on the TV news about crazies and whatsoever. Is that it? Anywhere you can find crazies."

"Did you notice something about Pike Place?" Tzaro directed the question to Carmody the city dweller and Wilson the sometime visitor. They both considered a moment.

"Not busy for a Sunday," the professor said. "It's the retail drop-off story, widely covered. There's no clear reason, apparently. Nothing financial, no fundamental."

"You'd expect the market to be swamped. And the train. Yes, a Sunday, but I counted maybe a dozen riders heading in, almost none coming back."

"So, business is slow," Svetla confirmed. "It's August. And you are saying..."

"He's saying something is making people stay away," Morgan explained.

"It's in the message, every second they're hitting Wundrus. And other sites, I think."

"Yes, I've heard about your theory. So why don't you just tell the Wundrus guys?"

"Because then whoever is doing this will know we know."

"If the stakes are as you say, and these events are related," Carmody said, "it's a logical inference."

"No one I know is a special paranoid. They're out there getting around. That asshole guy, maybe. Although... we're here talking about this. Why aren't *we*... infected?"

"Are you a social networker?" Tzaro asked. "A Wundrus Wun?"

She shook her head.

"How about Ping? Uptake?" He checked around the table although he didn't need to. "This is us." He picked up Morgan's ancient phone, which was on the table only in case Therica returned her call. "Marginals. Misfits. Out of the visible spectrum and, to use a phrase older than this venerable Galaxy, *under the radar.*"

Carmody chuckled. "I confess I have little use now for professional networking sites, but if I were your age, I imagine I would do it. But I wouldn't like it. Something in me will die with the personal defense of a thesis in the same room with the mind that created it, and the weight and smell of a volume in my hands."

"Sparky is right," Wilson said. "We're all the same tribe. No enemy. But maybe no friend."

"Friend!" Morgan laughed. "That's apropos, chief. Hey, friend me or leave me."

"So you have no help," Svetla put it to Tzaro. "What do you do? Do you have money?"

"What for?"

"To buy help. Some computer programming person. Find the hacker, right?"

"Okay, easy to do. They're all over the Net. But because of who they are, they're going to be altered, corrupted to some degree, incidental to total. Plus, I know none of them, and if this is international—Dongba is Chinese, correct? Or a rogue state or an entity that doesn't want its little intervention exposed...I can't take a chance with this."

"So I'm repeating myself. What do you do?"

Tzaro wanted to ask his Bulgarian hostess to refrain from further questioning. He wondered what it would be like to become silence. Not yet. But they all sat in silence. Carmody broke it.

"I happen to know a *developer*. I thought they were *programmers* or *coders*, but I assume somewhere along the line they became rebranded—a language event. In any case, I believe this person isn't likely to be one of 'them'.

"We were in the same class at Berkeley, and we were dating the same young woman. Rather, I dated her first. I recall taking her to a concert—the Starship, after they had been the Jefferson Starship."

"No way!" Morgan was delighted.

"Indeed. My friend Wes was there too, alone. In retrospect, I think he planned the whole thing. That's how they met. Jonquil soon wound up with him. I think she sensed a coder had better prospects than a student of archaeology. I abruptly stopped listening to the Starship. Ha!

"Jonquil eventually picked up the scent of a more promising hopeful in finance, a splendid choice. So much for the counterculture.

"Wes Englehart and I have stayed in contact. He resides in Portland. We get together when he's up here once a year or so, and whenever I'm down in that Neverland."

"Sorry, Cal, I appreciate the offer, but I'm sure you can agree whoever is behind this is bleeding edge, very sophisticated. I don't know where we could find a team—"

"I understand what you're saying." Carmody nodded deferentially then looked up in his clear-eyed way that seemed to resolve all doubt. "But Wes is ... *singularis*. Extraordinary. Granted, he's my age, and I'm sure many may be more nimble in the computer languages of the day, but he's really quite accomplished. He has the craft to proceed by instinct, and insight. Something like your Native American friend here."

"Thank you, Sparky." Wilson grinned.

"Besides," Carmody said, "I fail to see the alternative."

CHAPTER 12 A PROMISE

Tzaro tapped the numbered circles, took a breath, and held it for a count of three. If Lauren answered, he would handle it like an interview, smile while speaking. If voicemail, he would be brief but upbeat.

He had migrated to a far corner of the loft to call, opposite the quarters of Mara and Marco, which he imagined were empty. He was staring at the far corner of the long floor where Morgan and Svetla remained at the table. Three rings.

"Hello?"

Tzaro heard the sweet note of anticipation.

"Hi there."

"Dad! I thought you were … I thought you might call earlier."

"I know, sorry. I'm in Seattle and I had to be in a meeting when we usually talk. I should have texted you. What have you been up to?"

"Not much."

Tzaro was listening for something else, he wasn't sure what. He knew his fear was probably unwarranted. Derek wasn't, but how many kids were? What would it sound like? He tried to recall Therica's tones, her pauses and inflections. He might know it if he heard it, but he was praying not to. He did hear a hint of apprehension, predictable.

"Have you been thinking about school?" He meant the rickety-feeling bridge from Chavez Elementary to Rosewood Middle.

"Kind of. How come you're in Seattle? What are you doing?"

Tzaro knew he was ducking the main issue, but at the same time, a feeling of delight glowed in him—Derek was asking about his world, sounding quite adult.

"I'm in meetings with some other people. One is a woman from the San Francisco area, another is a professor I had when I went to college here, and another is from a Native American tribe, the Tulalip. We're trying to figure out what's causing some things—phenomena."

"Earthquakes?"

"Like that. I'm explaining my ideas. We know other people, some powerful people, have different ideas."

"Are you having an argument?"

"Not exactly. But we're all trying to decide who's right. And it takes some long meetings to decide that."

"Could the others be right?"

"It's possible," he said, readjusting to the fairly recent perception that dad may not be right in every foreseeable situation. "But I don't think so."

"Will the professor tell you who's right?"

"No, it's more like a democracy."

"Like everybody votes."

"That's right."

"And what if you don't win? Is it like worth it?"

"It's about finding out the truth. Truth is important, right? Everything depends on it, doesn't it? If we still believed things that weren't true, we could be treating diseases with toad soup and never traveling to other countries because we could fall off the edge of the world." For no reason he could explain, he was re-envisioning the decal on his bathroom mirror in college days: No False Prophets. "So if you believe something, it's worth standing up for what you think. The truth is better for everybody, even though they might not know it at the time." He wondered which of them he was really trying to convince. He could hear Derek's wheels turning.

"Are you still coming down like you said? To do the walk around…"

It was music to dad's ears. He had returned to the topic of school in his own way.

"Absolutely. Labor Day weekend. I'll be there on Saturday."

"Will you be done with your meetings?"

"By definition. Meaning yes, I'll be done. And we'll go to Rosewood and walk around, get the feel of it." They had walked the grounds of Chavez Elementary too, at the end of the summer before Derek started. The second time would be a tradition.

"Excel!" said his son in the vernacular.

"Right on."

"What?"

Tzaro went on to propose that they throw some also, which included practice pitches while Derek hit—an irresistible, he knew. They covered the Angels slump, nine out of first with less than a month to go. And to keep the fabric as whole as it could be, he asked about Derek's mom, who was there in the house's rambling spaces which they had both signed for in a previous lifetime. Did he want to talk to her? He would call her later.

"Hey, one more thing. This sounds funny but it's important. I don't want you to do Wundrus or Ping for a while, okay?"

"Why?"

"They have a really bad hacker virus. It's ruining people's computers, Zems like yours too. It will be safe soon. I'll let you know, okay?"

"Okay, Dad."

"You promise? This is really important."

"Yes." Tzaro heard the right note of gravitas. "I promise."

"Hey, call or text me whenever. I may be in meetings but I'll get back to you." He was thinking of no phone, checking his data with Morgan's. "And I'll call you as usual next Sunday."

Tzaro was staring across the floor of the old factory, becoming aware of the rooms of Sheetrock with bead-curtained doors, like a zoom pulling him back ineluctably into his strange new world.

"Love you too," he was saying.

As he headed back toward his room, Svetla came striding toward him purposefully. "We're going to take my car," she said.

"Sorry?"

"I drive. It's thirty-five each to cover gas and time. All right?"

"Sorry, I'm not—"

"Thirty. Last offer."

To Tzaro's relief, Carmody was coming up behind her.

"I just spoke with Wes Englehart," he said, twinkles in his eyes. "He's offered to assist."

Another detour. He was weighing the odds of any payoff while Therica's clock was ticking. How much did he believe he was right? Was it worth it?

"As I said, he's something of a paragon in his field. This young lady is suggesting—and I strongly recommend that you consider—leaving for Portland in the morning."

"You'll take us down," Tzaro said, imagining a dead end, stranded in Portland. "Back also?"

"You are such an American," she accused him with dark eyes, high eyebrows, but a smile tugging at the corners of her mouth. "Baby steps," she said and turned, trotting away at her sidewalk speed in polka dot tights. "Just get moving."

CHAPTER 13   JUNKERS

"Hey, I want to thank you," Tzaro said as they hustled across the street to Svetla's car. Breakfast of one old-fashioned doughnut had not raised his consciousness to morning level. Striding was unkinking his back from the air mattress. "For driving us, I mean. This interrupts your usual business, I'm sure." Interrupts yes, he was thinking, but one trip, five fares. Could be worse.

"No, is good timing. Let the smokes clear." He guessed she meant her crazed ex. "What about you, divorced?"

"Uh, yeah."

"Thought so. You have that way-far look in your eyes."

"Faraway look?"

"That's it. Why? Why did you divorce?"

He considered fending off the question, but on Svetla, impertinence was disarming.

"I guess we stopped laughing at each other's jokes."

So his faraway look was obvious, at least to their driver, although it had little to do with Lauren.

"Hi, dear. Were you happy with your session? A positive response?" Professor Carmody was on his phone behind Tzaro and Svetla. He listened for a moment, went on.

"Excellent, that's wonderful. Listen, I'm going to be in Portland for a couple of days. Yes, Tzaro Janssen is in town and we're going down to see Wes. I think so, yes. I expect we'll stay a couple of days, so I should still be able to pick you up. If it's going to be longer, I'll call. Love you."

"Cal, whenever you need to get back—"

"Look out!" Wilson shouted. His outstretched arm corralled both Tzaro and Carmody, sweeping them toward the curb. Tzaro tried to grab Svetla, but she had already reacted and pulled Morgan between parked cars. Tzaro went down on the curb, scrambled up.

"Jesus!" Morgan spat.

Tzaro only saw it when it was well past, a broad sedan, silent, eerie, black junker. He guessed it had missed them by six feet, and it rolled on, dumbly, constant speed. The trajectory was diagonal, across the opposite lane, suicidal.

In the middle of the block it jumped the curb, flattening a vending machine that popped its junk like confetti, and led with its left headlight into a concrete wall. It caromed off, straddled the sidewalk, and died. Halfway down the block, a gaunt geezer with a white beard pushing a shopping cart froze.

"My goodness," Carmody panted, Wilson's hand still on his back.

"Freaking insane," Morgan added, peering at the dumb machine that had nearly mowed them down.

"Probably drunk," Tzaro said, "or stoned."

"Or perhaps expired," Carmody added.

They observed it, sideways on the walk, no motion visible inside.

Tzaro and Wilson advanced cautiously and the others followed. The pilgrim with his shopping cart of belongings took off toward the opposite side of the street.

"This is some BS trick..." Svetla said when they were close enough to see inside.

Tzaro was expecting to see the driver slumped down or over, heart attack victim or stoner. Instead he was seeing empty seats. No driver or passengers.

"No accident," Wilson said and pointed to the GPS III console. "Manual override disabled."

"Robocar, humans locked out," Tzaro said. "Bad combination."

"What I said," Svetla affirmed.

"Do you think that guy?" Morgan asked.

"He is SOB but would not try to kill someone." Svetla picked up one of the pink robotic bunnies from the exploded machine. Its ears moved and one eye was tracking Tzaro.

Carmody wanted to make a report, but Tzaro persuaded him against it. It could take hours, and they needed every minute.

They reached Svetla's Grand Marquis and she clicked it open.

"Watch yourself," Wilson intimated to Morgan as they climbed in. "Eyes in front and behind."

"I took another couple, same drive, Seattle to Portland," Svetla told Wilson who was in the front passenger seat because he had the longest legs. They were rolling on I-5 well south of Olympia with the AC on high. The August sun was already in charge by ten, steam rising from the overnight rain. "They had to have a driver. Their honeymoon, right? This guy her husband kept singing ninety-nine beer bottles. By the time I dropped them, she wanted a divorce, I'm telling you."

"The first time I heard that song was in high school, Tahoma High. It's a kid's song you sing in summer camp, right? We didn't have summer camp, just camp. Camp counselor was drunk." Wilson grinned and didn't.

"You made it though, man," Morgan sent from the back against the door, "camp or no camp. You've got what, a couple acres of waterfront, and a cool boat."

Wilson was quiet. They were out of the hills into flat land, bright water west of them in the distance. The hum of the highway wrapped a radio band of country music and static.

"Made it?" he mused. "In some ways. Lucky in some ways. I want to do something else, you know? Back home, the reservation. My sister never made it out. I want to do something back there."

"You can, then," Svetla confirmed. "Just put your mind to it and follow your mind. All the great teachers say this. How do you think I survived when I came to the states? You can do whatsoever."

"Very admirable, Svetla, yes indeed," Carmody added from the back between Tzaro and Morgan. "I hope you'll consider returning to university."

"I sound big, don't I?" she said. "But not really."

Five in the car, Tzaro thought. It reminded him of car trips as a kid, when people did that. There were four then. He thought of Tilda in Northfield. He needed to call her. A sulfur smell was hitting the car as they passed a river town. A pulp mill, he guessed. Kalama, a little above the Columbia River.

Were they just wasting time? This Wes, who was he? Was he going to go head-to-head with legions of cyberpunks with their coding chops and genius apps? Yes, he wrote *Quetzal-Calc*, the 3-D end of the spreadsheet, incorporating probabilities, human factors, fuzzy logic. Made his fortune, and immortality of a kind. But this is now. The road ran both ways. There was a chance to turn it all around. Carmody sat next to him in the middle, almost shoulder-to-shoulder. Maybe he should quiz him for more about Wes. But the professor looked happy, maybe musing on Svetla's potential, or the potential of all. No point, Tzaro concluded. They were committed.

He closed his eyes and ran over it all—Therica, the manda-la wheel, San Diego and Bethesda, the Dongba pictograms. He could run it a thousand times but couldn't escape the question—what if he was wrong?

Air the only element moving, the box fan in the middle of her studio floor. Air feathering them, sweating and spent. On her night stand, hash pipe floating on lace. Open window past the foot of the bed. Edging toward evening but hours of light to go.

Name the poem and the poet.

"Marbles of the dancing floor
Break bitter furies of complexity."

The most he could come up with and more.

"Byzantium, Yeats. Ee-zee!"

She is watching the ceiling. He is watching her.

"Mark the ravening aspect of the moon,
her theater a threshing floor that terror froze."

Stunning. Incapacitating. From the lips just tasted.

"Plath. Something something."

"No-oh," she baritoned. "Amy Clampitt. Medusa."

"Oh right, but of course. How esoteric—"

Propped on her elbow, over him grinning. Fingertips light on his chest.

Her apartment that summer, Evanston just under Skokie. Her Northwestern Masters in Journalism. A workshop on writing for translation, instant connection, a few moments in Hyde Park, then talking their heads off all the way north on the Ravenswood el. Their first time.

"In one quarter mile, turn left on Burnside Avenue."

Tzaro snapped awake. They were on Portland's Eastside, rolling to a stop at a light. GPS was talking, and then there was no talking.

"Leave me alone!"

Tzaro heard but didn't process. He was spinning up from a former lifetime, not parsing language.

"Leave me alone!" came again sharply, a voice of desperation.

Across the street on the opposite sidewalk, a wiry male half-crouched beside a bike rack, shouting, spring-loaded, a hatchet in his hand. Svetla dropped the window a few inches.

"Leave me alone!" He shouted again and again, same volume, like a kid in a tantrum. Fifty feet from him on the sidewalk, a stocky matron with copper-tinted hair stood frozen, a toddler in tow.

"Leave me alone!"

The nanny pulled on the little boy's hand then wrapped his shoulder, dragging him back.

The shouter fell silent, turned to his objective. He bounced the hatchet in his hand, rotated it. His first blow, hatchet head to bike lock, was measured. Having gauged the target, he hit again and then again with both hands, furious strikes, metal sparking, a controlled frenzy of blows. The lock burst into pieces on the sidewalk.

He checked both directions then lifted the bike from its slot. Hatchet in hand, he mounted and rode away in the direction the neo-nanny had come.

Tzaro knew what he had seen.

"He's another," he said. The sound of his own voice chilled him.

Morgan seemed to understand then, and so did Wilson. Svetla turned back with her dark eyes, now childlike.

A horn sounded behind them. Green light.

"Yes, well," Carmody said into the silence as they began to move, "turn left at the next light as our virtual Virgil instructed. It isn't far now."

CHAPTER 14   WES

They followed Burnside for several blocks then turned left onto Ankeny. They found themselves in a neighborhood of comfortable Portland homes—rhododendron crowding broad porches, triple-sash windows, top-floor dormers. Soon GPS was talking them onto a narrow strip of blacktop into what appeared to be a forest.

"Meaning this?" Svetla sounded dubious.

"Yes, this is it," Carmody confirmed. "It's unmarked."

The Grand Marquis nosed into the woods, filling the drive. The asphalt gave way to white gravel.

"Is this a park or something…" Morgan trailed off as they rounded a bend and the woods opened into a clearing. In the middle stood a spreading two-story house, white frame, with a farmhouse porch the width of the first floor.

"It's huge," Svetla gushed.

A single cupola stood another story high. When they reached the grand apron at the end of the drive, they halted before a Victorian matron, Queen Anne style, fluted columns framing the broad porch, white gingerbread brackets.

"It's like a big dollhouse," she added.

"Somebody's fantasy," Morgan said.

"Quite," the professor confirmed. "Let's go in."

Carmody rang the bell twice then pulled the screen, which was the only door separating them from the foyer. He stepped inside and motioned them to follow.

"Hello, Wesley, it's Cal. We're here."

Tzaro heard stirring upstairs above the high-ceilinged entry, capacious and cool. Stairs rose to his left, and to his right in the living room he could make out a stuffed sofa and chairs, furnishings from an age gone by.

"Hello, yes. Coming." The eager-sounding voice came from above, and then Wes Englehart was on the stairs.

Amish of the islands, was Tzaro's first impression. Gray beard, no mustache, Hawaiian shirt worn out over khaki shorts, huaraches.

"So glad you could come," he greeted them at the bottom of the stairs. As they made their introductions, Tzaro noticed his glance drop to the floor or shift sideways behind his glasses. Distracted, Tzaro thought, a mad scientist air about him.

"Come in, please," he said, stepping into the high, half-dark space of the living room. No motion sensors. He switched on an old brass floor lamp.

"You must be thirsty after your long drive. What can I...We have cran elixir, cold mead...Yes?"

"Oooh," Svetla purred. In the far corner sat what appeared to be an old Wurlitzer jukebox, a facade of plastic columns and a middle arch, magically glowing yellow, red, and blue.

"That's two meads, one cran, and a water." Wes headed for the kitchen. Before Carmody followed, Tzaro stopped him.

"Tell him his fly's open," he said, thinking, *Jesus.*

"May I?" Svetla asked Wes. He and Carmody were returning with bottles. "My parents have one. A record player." She was referring to the Wurlitzer, which was not a jukebox but a cathedral with a latter-day altar, a turntable. She held up an ancient square album cover—black and white and pink—*Surrealistic Pillow*.

Wes was delighted. Svetla centered the vinyl platter expertly and triggered the turntable arm.

Carmody launched into the backstory for Wes, and Morgan shuffled around by the piano, stretching her legs. Also too stiff to sit, Wilson stood eye-to-eye with a huge barn owl on a ledge, its wings spread. A brass plate on its stand said "Thor."

Most of the wall above the sofa was covered with a framed print—Jasper Johns' tiled American flags. Tzaro considered sitting but standing felt too good.

And all the joy within you dies

He had to admit, Wes's old style felt comfortable. But by any sane standards, he was as marginal as the rest of them, probably more, when it came to scoping the haunted zones of the social network.

Svetla was emoting and lip-synching to a bust of Beethoven on the bookcase.

Don't you want somebody to love?

Tzaro chugged the cold mead, Therica tumbling through his thoughts. Something rubbed against his right leg above the ankle and he started—the hip of a cat, a Siamese with a purple head.

"May I..." Wes said in the space between tracks, "show you your rooms? I'm sure you'd like to unpack your things ... Svetla, Morgan, and Tzaro," he added, nodding toward each in turn. Without waiting for a response, he headed toward the stairs. Tzaro took note. While appearing terminally distracted, he had cached all their names.

The four bedrooms on the second floor each had a brass nameplate, like an annex of Hotel California. Wilson took Lennon. Carmody chose Carole King. Tzaro took Dylan, and because it had two beds, Svetla and Morgan doubled up in The Byrds.

After settling in, Wilson and Morgan left for a walk around the grounds. Svetla put on George Harrison's *Cloud Nine* downstairs. Cal and Tzaro were alone with Wes.

"I'm convinced it's a real threat," Carmody put to his old friend. "Not a hoax or random mischief. The use of the mandala—trap door to the subliminal—and the pictographic message. Those are sophisticated choices, tactical."

"Do you have any idea who?" Wes nearly whispered, clearly hooked.

"Exactly what we need you to tell us, my dear genius. We have our theories. Tzaro, if you could summarize?"

"I'm the farthest thing from an expert, but given that they've compromised some of the highest trafficked sites in the world with security that must be peerless, the skill and resources are obvious. And if the intent is what I think it is— to incapacitate and trigger violence—then it's either cyber warfare with no single target, or zealots of whatever stripe turning the Western Internet against its profane creators. So possibly a rogue state, or extremists with intel and backing."

"And you've contacted the sites—"

"Impossible to trust. There's no way to know if they're being intercepted or if their developers might be involved, or altered like other victims."

"And Cal told me you went to the FBI."

"They think it's a prank and people are going nuts because they're eating rye fungus."

Wes stared at him. "Ergot?" His eyes tightened.

"Well, yeah, that's their cover for having no clue."

Wes pulled his beard then laughed in Tzaro's face. He turned to Cal and laughed, and Cal laughed back. Then they were all laughing, sharing the absurdity, laughter booming in the tall hallway. And then they were done.

Wes pushed his glasses up on his nose.

"Shall we get started?" he said. Tzaro started to thank him, but he was already out of the bedroom, heading for the stairs.

CHAPTER 15   MUSEUM OF THE TITANS

Back downstairs with Wes in the lead, Tzaro noted Svetla had moved on to Smokey and the Miracles—*The Tracks of My Tears*. She was dancing in the middle of the floor, bobbing and grooving as the Siamese watched from the sofa. He felt a prick of envy. She could afford the distance, on Therica and all of it. Past the kitchen, a few steps led to the basement door.

"Abandon hope, all ye who enter here," Carmody tossed over his shoulder to Tzaro as Wes pulled the door.

A complex aroma of mildew and electronics met them. Wes's computer lab looked more like a swap meet of e-junk. Dim light emanated from half a dozen screens. On the closest, a band of colors cycled above a waveform that reminded Tzaro of a seismograph.

"Portrait of a sleeping brain," Wes explained. "It's a proto-type for Johns Hopkins. They want to be able to track and interact with people when they dream, anywhere in the world. This subject is in Stockholm."

"Male or female?" Tzaro asked.

Wes poked a key and a photo popped into a corner of the window. A thirty-something woman, not a typical Swede, dark skinned—Middle Eastern, Tzaro thought, probably a refugee from some raging corner of the caliphate.

On the wall behind the table crowded with monitors hung a pair of wanted posters—one for *QuetzalCalc* with the resplendent bird logo, the other for a game, *Zoners*, programmers Wes Engelhart and Bill Darrah.

"While you're here, don't miss the Museum of the Titans." Tzaro didn't see Wes flip the switch, only the cones of light that dropped onto a semicircle of ancient computers at the rear of the room. Clearly he needed to share the exhibit. Tzaro could imagine visitors might be few, more like guests at Bates Motel. They strolled back.

"Atari 800," Wes said, pointing to a flattish tan box with an external floppy drive. "Commodore 64." The Titans numbered at least a dozen. "Remember the chiclet keyboard? IBM PC. And," he said reverentially, "the Amiga. The prototypes were in balsa wood boxes. Take your time. Fire them up if you want. They all run. Ah!" His index finger went up. "Wundrus," he said, recalling his mission, drifting away. "Wundrus."

Little brass nameplates, Tzaro saw, like Thor's and the ones over the bedroom doors. Sinclair ZX-81. Amstrad. North Star Horizon.

"Wes is the embodiment of all this," Carmody said. "It's all cached in his memory, where access has always been random. Ha!" He tapped the chiclet keyboard, and the command line glowed green on the CRT monitor. "The languages are like his second tongue. Ancient languages now, no doubt. We're partners in antiquity.

"But he isn't limited. As we know, language prepares us for language, contours our learning. His gift is a kind of thinking, a special blend of capabilities and insight that he brings to problems. Have faith—you will be rewarded."

As they left the museum to seek out their genius, Tzaro wanted to believe, but the other side rushed in. He needed to set a limit, put Wes on a timer. How he was going to do that, he had no idea. But he was thinking of the magnitude of the challenge, the cost of failure, and close to home, of Therica and Derek. If the experiment with Wes proved to be a dead end, cutting it off should be a top priority.

They followed in the direction Wes had gone and rounded a baffle that partitioned a section of the basement. Here was moonglow of a different hue, one screen with a copper desktop, a scatter of icons silver and white. The other screen in front of Wes was split, Wundrus in one pane, Tzaro's capture, which Carmody had sent him, in the other.

In front of his oversized laptop, to the side of his screen and keyboard was another brass nameplate.

"R.B.?" Tzaro asked.

"Rocky Balboa," Wes clarified. "He's ruggedized. You can roll him down the stairs from the second floor. I did when I got him—an acid test of the vendor's claims."

"How can we help?" Carmody offered, pulling up a chair.

Wes's chair was an enormous charcoal bat form with a NASA insignia on the back. Tzaro's eye went to the ceiling—a projection that covered the twenty-by-twenty like the Sistine ceiling—the earth from space, Apollo 17, the luminous blue orb gauzed in white, unique, fragile-looking, and alone.

"Need to check..." Wes started. He clacked off a run on the keyboard and the copper screen scrolled white text. Dr. Dobbs Index was the window title.

"Pud-zee," he said and the screen rolled.

"September! About a year..."

He started into a stack of magazines on the floor at the end of his desk. He clutched a chunk of issues to his chest and picked the next one off the top.

"Yes!" He sat back down and rotated his chair to face them both.

Tzaro recognized the name of the magazine, *Dr. Dobbs Journal.* The cover was a splash of carroty gold over columns of indented code. It was clear to Tzaro that clarification would be painful for Wes at the moment.

"And to your question, dear Calvin..." Wes was spinning back, retrieving from RAM, as he had done with the names. "You can help by leaving. Ha! But leave your phone on. This may take a while."

"We copy," Carmody said. "We shall do. We wish you all the best. Your dinner?"

"Turkey Expando and Tofu Taters. The top freezer drawer. Thank you so." Wes rotated in his chair, its profile like a Stealth bomber, and began flipping into *Dr. Dobbs Journal*.

Tzaro followed his professor out of the copper and white light, past the hall of digital relics, and tried to focus on the idea that trust itself had value, regardless of its subgenre, which in this case reminded him uncomfortably of the one known as blind faith.

"I could have danced all night," Svetla warbled and pirouetted in the bedroom while Morgan regarded her like an alien. "I could stay here forever."

From his spot in the door, Tzaro found her delightful.

"Bad old jukebox...okay," Morgan admitted. "Killer tunes, classics all, I'm sure. But reality check here. We're so losing time. We need a real coder or maybe a lot of coders who aren't already wonky or from another century—"

"Haven't we been here before?" Tzaro said. "What am I missing?"

"Some NGOs have major IT presences. They use vendors, consultants—"

"And we'd be starting cold, right? Wes is here now, and he has chops."

"He's a cool old guy, but come on! How many paranoid psychos are coming online every minute? And Therica—"

"All right! I hear you." His volume surprised them all into a moment of silence.

"We're on the same page here. Cutoff is tomorrow evening. Something actionable from Wes or we start over." He tried to sound conciliatory, downshifting. "Maybe you could make some calls."

"Okay. Yeah, I could do that."

They nodded and Tzaro was happy to leave the door and decamp to the refuge of his own room.

On his back in the dark, he considered whether there was an investment in life more satisfying than a ceiling fan. The rotation lifted him to a place between earth and memory. Derek first. Text him on Morgan's phone. No Wundrus, or any others. Therica. Her parents, what it would be like to tell them. He tried to breathe through that one, hoping as closely as he could come to praying he would never have to. And then...

Rolling into the West Side in narcotic summer, evening's long blue spell. Mustang radio cranked up, wind whipping their hair, her one bare foot on the dashboard.

Chicago blocks clickety-clacking into haze, the flat hour you could drive west without nearing the city limit.

Passing Chicago Circle campus, then Little Italy, *Born to Run* on the oldies. Angling to a hot dog stand lit like a county fair around Harrison and Kedzie.

Jumbo polish sausage, the first bite paradisal. Her face bright, stars in her eyes under cones of white light.

Woofer booms and salsa anthem blasting from the street behind them. Retro, Ruben Blades. *Tres muchachos* cruising in a shovel-nosed Cougar, yellow and chrome.

CHAPTER 16 PUD-Z

yo. can u talk?

In a few seconds, Tzaro saw cycling dots and then text.

ya ya!

"Hi there."

"Dad! What's up? Are you in a meeting?"

"No, on a business trip. You're at camp, right? Is Mom coming?" The idea of math camp made Tzaro recoil; it was Lauren's idea.

"Yeah, she'll be here in like ten minutes probably."

Tzaro heard voices in the background, random concussions. Basketball. One of the structured activities. Derek was waiting in the gym.

"I just wanted to make sure about something."

"What?"

"You know what we talked about Sunday?"

"You mean about Wundrus? You said not to go there."

"Right, great. So you haven't?"

"I promised, right?"

Tzaro was relieved to hear the note of annoyance. It was the reassurance he had been after.

"Ping either, okay?"

"How long do you think? Brandon put assignments on Spritely."

Bought in, Tzaro thought, even the school district, up to their eyeballs.

"Please ask Brandon to give them to you another way. He could print—"

"Dad, everybody else—"

"Do you want me to ask him?"

"No."

"So you'll ask him?"

"Yeah."

"Thank you. And I'll let you know as soon as the coast is clear." He sounded ancient with the phrase, he knew, but he let it go. "How's it going otherwise?"

"It's good, I'm on top of it."

"You sure? You sound...not so sure."

"It was kind of weird today. A lot of kids didn't come. Some note is going home to parents. Is it something about Wundrus?"

"Could be. We have our agreement, right?"

"Right. She's here."

It ran through him, a rod of memory.

"Okay, look...tell Mom too."

"Okay."

"Love you."

Tzaro crossed the living room to Morgan and placed her phone on the dining room table. She received it without a nod. She was on one of the laptops, checking nonprofit leads to programmers, he assumed. For a moment he imagined retrieving it. He doubted she would even notice. Six-seven-eight, eight-seven-four, twenty-three thirty. But the timing was nuts, he realized, vaguely grasping that it was evening in

Atlanta. Of course it was, family time, and that was as good an excuse as any not to call.

The living room of Wes's commodious house shared the vibe of the August day that seemed endless. Becalmed. Professor Carmody had returned from a hike around the grounds with praise for the apple and pear orchard. Between a shower and dinner, he was reading Wes's copy of *The Lathe of Heaven* in a chair in the corner, the purple cat at his feet.

Wilson was upstairs. Tzaro regretted having entangled him. He seemed subdued, out of his element.

Svetla was curled on the sofa, throw pillows under her head, the TV across from her on low.

They were all in a limboid state, suspended, purgatorial. They were waiting for Wes, who had not surfaced for meals since the day before.

Tzaro worked his way over to Svetla and it was as he suspected. She was out, a soccer match on the TV, barely audible. He viewed the livid green field, no way he could relate. He didn't want to speak so he was happy to see the remote. He slipped it off the sofa and punched. A Nepraltha class action suit ad. Punched again.

The Asian reporter from KATU News looked familiar, but he didn't know her name. Looking ill at ease, the interviewee stood in front of one of Portland's red streetcars. The shot cut to a car rolling on the Tenth Street line. He raised the volume to audible.

"...trend, is that right?"

"We have had lower ridership on all the lines for the last six weeks. That's contrary to the trend we had been seeing. For example, the Third Street addition was in response to increasing demand." The Portland Transit spokesman shifted his weight from one foot to the other.

Third Street Trolley Project Halted overlaid the bottom of the screen. The lady with the mic leaned in.

"And in the last several days, you've seen a noticeable drop-off?"

"Our ridership this week compared to a year ago is down forty-one percent." The guy reminded Tzaro of a high school kid in a science fair who couldn't wait to wrap his project summary and sit down.

"The same, right?" Morgan was beside him suddenly, laptop folded under her arm.

"It looks that way."

The professor was watching too, book in his lap.

"Let's get out of here," she said, cadence falling, beyond patience.

"We said end of the day."

"It's almost four. What end? Workday? Minute to midnight? What's the point?"

"I told Wes he has all of today," Carmody joined in.

"Professor, I appreciate that he's your friend, but we have a friend who's in need of our help. Now. You didn't see her, we did. I mean no disrespect. You obviously care a great deal about people. But I have to help her."

"Yes, Morgan, I hear your concern," Carmody said. "And I understand the urgency, for her and others. But I do believe our best option is here in this house. I know you're skeptical, you have every right to be. But as I can never know your friend, I suggest you can't know Wes as I do."

"Blind faith." Morgan said it. Tzaro had to remind himself that he didn't.

"Who's winning?" Svetla sat up groggily.

"Sorry." Tzaro clicked back to the field of green. "Is Bulgaria playing?"

"No, some Germans. They don't know soccer."

"I need to make some calls," Morgan said and headed upstairs.

Tzaro stared into the soccer match, immobilized. He didn't care to look the professor in the eye.

"I'd like to check in with him," he said.

He could see Carmody processed the subtext. On the way to the basement Tzaro was tight, trying to fabricate a way to let Wes off the hook with their sincere thanks. Past the kitchen he took the steps down to the basement door.

"Jesus!" The door swung open and Wes nearly blundered into him. "I didn't expect—"

"No. Yes!" Wes's face seemed to glow, as though his copper screen had glazed him. "It's pudzee," he said, the twinkle back behind his glasses. Tzaro detected he could use a shower.

"Really."

"Are the others—"

"The living room."

Tzaro called upstairs to Morgan and Wilson. Wes launched in without waiting.

"Pudzee, indeed it was the September issue." He held up the *Dr. Dobbs Journal.* "That's P-U-D-Z. A word game—anagrammatic spin on UDP, User Datagram Protocol. It was one of the first Internet protocols, 1980 or so, Dave Reed's baby. It was the fastest of all because of no error checking, no checksum. It's been refactored by a scrum of Siberians." He showcased the magazine cover, the feature story: *Russian Fireball—The New UPD.* "They added the 'Z'. It's the new 'X'."

"Russians," Morgan said from the door.

"A mystery," Wes said.

"Wrapped in a puzzle," Carmody continued.

"Inside ... an enigma!" Wes finished and they laughed heartily. Tzaro vaguely recognized the epigram—Churchillian, from the prior century.

"How do you know?" Tzaro asked.

"Packet cleaning. It intercepts packets, cleans them, inserts a packet, and closes. Ingeniously, seamlessly, stitches up. Like a perfectly implanted cellular enhancement. No rejection. Because no checksum, you see."

"Russian," Morgan said again and stared at them all, eyebrows raised. It occurred to Tzaro that she was waiting for them to get it, as though she had turned a Tarot card face up.

"Classified," he said. "Of course."

The realization sank through him, and he recognized it in Morgan's face. He checked Carmody, and in the next moment it was there too. To Wes it would mean little or nothing, his riddle, the part of it he could see, having been solved.

"It's why we got crap from Patel." Tzaro played it through. "Rye fungus, cat virus."

"All smoke," Morgan said.

"You're suggesting this is cyber warfare," Carmody said.

"They're cloaking it," Tzaro said. "Top secret."

"And the FBI agreed to an interview because you had—"

"Primo evidence," Morgan finished.

"Why doesn't the FBI just take those sites down?" Carmody asked.

"It's not that easy," Wes said. "Sites like this have mirror servers all over the world."

"They're keeping it quiet until they have enough on them to move," Morgan went on. "International has to be in on it too, maybe Interpol."

On this level, Tzaro understood, they were out of their league. Only pawns, maybe less. They were little peddlers spinning their wheels.

"Thank you," Tzaro said to Wes, who was looking downcast. "You set us straight. We can stop wasting time."

"You're quite right about that," Carmody added. "Indirection, yes, but you found direction out."

"Let's find Therica," Tzaro said to Morgan. "Maybe she's still on the island.

"Svetla, can you take us back in the morning?"

"Well," Svetla said, looking longingly at the Wurlitzer turntable, "I'm sorry to hear this. But," she said heading for the vintage vinyl, "time for a few more. Wes, what do you want to hear?"

CHAPTER 17   ZIGZAG

I said Doctor, Doctor, Mister M.D.
Can you tell me what's ailing me?
Svetla's choice, or it could have been Wes's, reached Tzaro on the second floor. The Rascals, *Good Lovin'*. He was heading for Wilson's door. Part of him was glad to be letting the big man off the hook.

"Hey, in the morning we're going to break camp. So to speak." Wilson was filling the length of his bed, sandals off, more at rest than sullen as Tzaro had imagined. "Wes determined it's cyber warfare, over our heads. Apparently the tech is a specialty of Russian hackers. It looks like the FBI is covering it up until they have a clear shot. It's nothing we're going to fix."

He expected some sign of relief, but instead Wilson seemed oddly disappointed.

"Do you believe that?"

It felt like Wilson was peering into him, seeing inside, picking up on something he was refusing to admit.

"I'd be crazy not to, right?"

Wilson studied him a moment.

"Hold on, boss." He sat up abruptly. "I think you're getting in your own way." He slipped on his sandals. "Let's take a walk.

Wilson led out the back door into the yard that he and Morgan had explored the day they arrived. It was after four-thirty with the sun still beating, into the nineties. They crossed the open lawn at least fifty yards to the first shade under an umbrella of old oaks.

He unzipped a pocket in the leg of his khakis and produced a thin-stemmed wooden pipe with a colored bowl. Next he opened a Ziploc of vegetable matter, darker and solider looking than pot.

A bird screamed somewhere overhead and Wilson spotted him.

"Red tail," he said. "*My place*, he says. *This is my place.*" He pinched from the bag and filled the bowl and tamped it down.

"A little warm for this?" Tzaro wiped his brow with the side of his thumb.

Wilson grinned then touched a lighter flame to the bowl and sucked a glow.

Tzaro slipped the smooth stem into his mouth. He took a tentative draw and tried to hold it down but coughed anyway. An acrid smoke taste, but not of pot.

"Is this peyote?" He felt a rush of circulation around his eyes. "Hash?"

Wilson finished his second draw.

"A special blend."

Tzaro's next was smoother.

"Why," he started when things were moving slower, "are we doing this? Not complaining, just curious."

Wilson passed the pipe and Tzaro saw for the first time the carved and painted images on the bowl. The iconic raven or orca. Salish style or Tlingit.

"So we can take another look."

Tzaro drew the vapors of vegetation in and shut the door of breath on them and held them down. Beyond their island of shade, heat shimmered above the grass, charged air more than itself, a viscous presence, plasmic.

We snatch ourselves away from time, he was nearly sure he said, *and time snatches us back.*

Soon he was crossing the yard again under the sun's heat that no longer pounded but embraced. He had the sense they had agreed to return to the house and go where Wilson had not been. He tried to identify any reason not to, but it was like trying to touch solid ground when his every step landed an inch or two above the spinning earth. Wilson was in the lead.

In the kitchen they switched places. Tzaro could smell hints of coffee and spice, and as he stepped down the two steps to the basement door, his own deodorant scent and sweat. He knocked twice. Wilson was a step behind him.

"Wes?" Tzaro called and turned the knob at the same time. Not locked. This time the smell of the humid, cool basement and electronics was nearly overwhelming. He was there to take Wilson to the image, that much he knew. Copperish light emanated from the corner, and he was leading the way in the dark.

Wes's screen was filled with three panels of code and one of Tzaro's screen capture. He clicked the mandala image to the front.

Wilson took Wes's astronaut wing chair in front of the monitor, and Tzaro rolled another chair beside him. As Wilson stared at the capture, Tzaro could sense him breathing. Tzaro focused on the image too, and concentration itself seemed new, total and pure, not as though he was seeing the image for the first time but through new eyes.

A bounding ring, silver, as though airbrushed with stardust. Within it an inscribed square, deeper red, four gold gates at the corners. Within that square floated another, gold, with black gates. In the center, the Dongba pictographs. For the first time Tzaro became aware of the texture of the green background, a kaleidoscopic mosaic of leaves, semitransparent and opaque. Though fixed, it seemed to rotate, the essence of rotation in stasis. Wilson was pointing at the screen.

In the lower right corner, Tzaro noticed a new asymmetry. All the corners were hatched with narrow diagonal bands, silver gray, like the bounding ring. But the ones in the lower right were segmented into sections separated by black borders. Each band bore a single colored subsection in black, red, or gold, like a bead on a string. Not random, Tzaro realized. A code, a pattern.

"Five lines," Wilson said, as though reading his mind.

With cool focus, Tzaro realized he could count the tiny subdivisions.

"Twenty-three," he said, "twenty-four…" They both sat in silence, processing. "Letters! The alphabet. Maybe, we don't know. And what about the colored ones…. Can you write out an alphabet—"

"Number the letters," Wilson finished. He dug for a pen in the back of a drawer. No paper. He used the back of a *Dr. Dobbs*.

Beginning with the innermost line, Tzaro counted the position of the first colored bead.

"Thirteen."

Wilson circled letter thirteen—M.

The next line was obvious.

"Three."

The bead on the next line was in the same position as the first.

"Thirteen. Twenty-two."

And the last was nearer the start.

"Nine."

They checked the circled letters. They spelled nothing. M, C, M, V, I.

"MC...what acronym?"

Neither of them could answer.

"M-C-M-V-I.

"Not letters!" Tzaro burst. "Numbers! Roman numerals. One thousand ... one thousand nine hundred six. What the freak is that?"

Wilson said nothing but started to hum quietly. In a moment Tzaro recognized the cadences of a chant. He went on for more than a minute. Then he was silent, rocking slightly, focused on the screen. Tzaro struggled to maintain his patience. The silence stretched across another minute that seemed endless. He could stand it no longer.

"What do you—"

Wilson pointed again, to the lower right quadrant, and drew his finger down and out to the corner.

In the background of translucent leaf shapes, cutting through it or under it, Tzaro detected a wavering darkness. It was a line pattern, darker gray by a few shades than the diagonal bands and the ring, a zigzag shape.

"What is it, lightning?" He checked the other corners. It was the only one.

Wilson sat, hulking and inert, then began the chant again, louder, his rich baritone riding the Tulalip chant in the cave of the images. And then he was silent.

No answer, Tzaro realized. He closed his eyes and tried to replay the chant he had heard in his head, tried to let it fill him. He needed to ride it out to the margin where it became smoke.

The zigzag lightning was like a bait skittering on the surface. It teased up images and patterns. He could have been dreaming, associating freely, lucidly, unconstrained by reason. When it came to him he was shocked. It had been so close to him all the time. It touched him, electric.

"Fault!" he expelled, eyes wide. Wilson stared at him. "It's a fault. A big one!"

Wes was in the lead in shorts and sandals, hair still wet, bath towel over his shoulders, as they descended again. Tzaro had apologized for rushing him post-shower, but he had to be sure.

"This is it, in the corner."

Wes adjusted his glasses, peered in.

"This jagged line and a Roman numeral. One thousand nine hundred six. As in 1906." Tzaro checked their wheels spinning. Nothing yet. "The zigzag represents the fault. As in San Andreas." He dragged out the pregnant pause like the good professor teasing out recognition. He detected a glimmer, their lights coming on. "The San Francisco Quake."

Wes chuckled, then Wilson.

"That's what they're saying, trust me. But how to take it? Some reference by Russian hackers to earth rattling, big shake-up, the big one, yada... Or I'm wondering... Did they get carried away with the graffiti here? Could it be there's another group besides the Russians, maybe a lot closer to home?" He scanned Wes for micro-responses. Was he offended? Skeptical? What was playing behind the glasses?

Wes leaned forward, clicked on the mic.

"Pudzee," he enunciated. A pane rolled with links. "Filter... San Francisco."

Three links remained.

"Thought I saw it..."

He clicked the one in the visited color. It was a tech blog, KBammer.

"...at Lawrence Livermore ... using PUD-Z in persistent advanced threat scenarios ... appropriated by the hack community, San Francisco and East Bay."

Tzaro didn't need to ask the question.

"Looks like there's a cell there," Wes said.

Upstairs, Tzaro found the women together in their room, Svetla regaling her roommate on the cost of lip gloss in America.

"Svetla," he said, "may we hire your conveyance for a few more days?"

They stared at him like the alien he was, outside the company of women and abruptly enthusiastic, bordering on possessed.

"We need to go to San Francisco."

CHAPTER 18   QUILL

Warm air whipped through the wide windows of the Grand Marquis. Going on seven, the sun still sat well above the horizon, and it would have been sweltering if they had been standing on the asphalt instead of hurtling over it. After the last gas stop, Svetla had cut the AC so they wouldn't have to stop again.

Six hundred thirty-five miles, her GPS read when they started, Portland to San Francisco. After almost eleven hours on I-5, it said sixteen.

She had told them at the start: at least two gas stops and eleven hours. Gas was either side of a buck with few guzzlers like Svetla's left on the road. The trick had been finding stations with a pump together with the chargers.

Wilson rode shotgun, inclined toward the window, dead to the world. In the back, Morgan sat behind Svetla, and Tzaro had the opposite window. Carmody and Wes were between them, talking old times much of the way, Wes with R.B. on his lap.

At the second fuel station, they had bought out the peanut butter crackers and wolfed all of them. Now they were sweaty and tired, in the home stretch and counting down the miles.

"How do I go in?" Svetla called to Morgan in the back.

"Keep going on 80. We'll be taking the Bay Bridge."

"El Cerrito," Wes read the sign and chuckled. "It's been a while."

"The Catacombs," Carmody recalled from their undergrad days.

"That was Berkeley."

"No way," Cal insisted, sounding halfway certain.

Tzaro looked out over the El Cerrito flats and the glittering bay. He could make out the beginnings of a serrated skyline in the glare of the low sun.

Where to start? Morgan their guide had her answer and he was willing to go with it. Market Street South, he was thinking from studying the map on her phone. That wasn't quite right... something Market.

He saw white tire smoke and brake lights before he heard the horns. A hundred yards or so in front of them in the inside lane, a bus was braking, fishtailing. Smoke clouded up from the blacktop. Cars screeched behind it. One swerved around.

Svetla came off the gas and held steady in the center lane. Wilson sat bolt upright, partially blocking Tzaro's view. As they passed the bus halted on the shoulder, Tzaro saw a heavyset woman lumbering away from the front, a younger man running behind quickly overtaking her.

He strained to see through the windshield of the bus. The driver's seat appeared to be empty. The man passed the woman with her hobbling gate. They both seemed to be running out of fear. The lanes of traffic normalized, rolled on, but the smell of burned rubber lingered.

"Those were ones, right?" Svetla called over her shoulder, sounding anxious, pumped with adrenaline. "Crazies like that guy in Portland?"

Tzaro nodded but she missed him in the mirror. No one else spoke.

"Take the exit to Fifth," Morgan said. All were sitting at attention as they descended into the city. The entry into San Francisco was not what Tzaro had been expecting. They had been focused on the Transamerica Pyramid and the rest of the skyline since Yerba Buena Island. Now they were on the skirmish line between industrial and modular urban. Buildings like stacks of cans in primary colors alternated with plumbing wholesalers and recyclers, pet shops, and plastic surgery clinics.

"Take a left here." They rolled on for a couple of blocks.

Tzaro read the street sign: Minna.

"This is it."

Svetla pulled over, and they piled out for the first time in three hours. They unfolded, groaning. Tzaro did squats and toe raises to restart his circulation. Wilson lumbered in a circle. Wes was bending and unbending, laptop to his chest. Carmody tried bouncing up and down like a piston. With her backpack strap over one shoulder, Morgan was heading for their destination.

The building sat in mid-block, a black concrete box with a steel door painted silver. A ball of chain link above the door dropped a blue cone of light. To the left of the door in white stencil lettering: Gasoline Valley. Morgan pulled the door and they went in.

Tzaro was engulfed in cool and dark, able to see only a few feet. He felt a dash of animal fear, a moment of disorientation, as though he could be a step or two from an edge. The air held a subterranean blend of aromas, alcohol and mixed smokes. Soon he could distinguish booths along the black walls. Two were dimly illuminated, he realized, by laptop screens. In front of one he could make out the hunched silhouette of an occupant.

"Hello," Morgan called. "Quill?"

The figure failed to react.

"Hey!" Svetla called and took off toward the booth. After a day-long drive, she clearly wasn't interested in patience. They all followed.

Tzaro expected to see a game, but the nerd's screen was crowded with code. He started when he became aware of them, and Tzaro could hear the music escaping from his earbuds.

"Hi, what can I..." He looked surprised and amorphously chunky in a black T that said *Ozoners* over an image of an ancient drive-in theater. His earbuds came off and Tzaro thought he detected Megadeth's "Symphony of Destruction," or a derivative. The laptop was surrounded with cans of Mountain Dew.

"Yes," Svetla continued. "My friend is looking for..." Morgan was at her side now.

"Quill. Is he around somewhere?"

In the presence of two interrogating females, his nose involuntarily wrinkled, lifting his upper lip. His gum had kept growing down over tiny teeth.

"I think I saw... I'll..."

He was out of the booth and shuffling toward the back. For the first time Tzaro noticed the low stage at the end of the room. The width of the wall behind it was covered with a photo of burning hills like ones he had seen before. He squinted to focus. Half a dozen pockets of orange flame nestled in deep green. Napalm.

"Mo! What's hap, babe?" Quill, lanky and a long-haired, met Morgan in the middle of the floor and they clinched.

"Watch out," she said. "I probably stink. We just did ten plus hours from Portland. If you could be so kind and resourceful—these poor folks need a place to crash."

Tzaro knew the story. Quill and Morgan were fellow activists, veterans of old campaigns, including the Silicon Valley appropriation of the once low-rent Tenderloin. Quill worked in the gray zone of security entrepreneurs. He was a defense contractor for enterprises under fire from cyber strikes. With *former hacker* declared on his resume, he had the cred. Undeclared, he might also play the other side selectively when it paid, like the others in his circle, a loose confederation of Dark Web talent that Morgan thought could hold a key.

They made their intros.

Quill was aptly named, slight but wiry. Anglo-Asian-looking, with black hair that fell curtain-straight. A good match for Morgan, Tzaro thought, although perhaps a couple of years younger.

"Not a problem—I've been holding your suite," he said. "The fob's at my place, it's on the way."

They departed Gasoline Valley with Quill in the lead on his electric bike and Morgan on the seat behind him. Svetla followed and they hung a left before the bridge onto a street called Mission, an occasional rip of a motorcycle and a blast of Bachata. They followed it another twenty minutes until the stucco houses began to thin out.

Morgan had said Quill lived off the grid. How far off, Tzaro didn't realize.

"So what is ..." Svetla was turning in, but she sounded nervous.

"Beautiful," Wilson said.

"It's what we refer to as a junkyard," Carmody confirmed. The chain-link gate slid open before Quill's bike.

They followed into the graveyard past eyeless and toothless wrecks. Quill pulled up outside a faded red bus, *Magic Bus* on the side in the loopy scroll of the kool-aid acid era. The roof appeared to be covered with solar panels, except for a cistern in the middle, and Tzaro noticed a fan of windmill blades in the back.

"You'd be welcome to stay here ..." He unlocked the fabricated steel door and it swung open, flooding them with heat. "But I imagine you'd prefer real beds."

From the top of the steps, Tzaro made out two cot-style pallets across from each other at the end of the aisle. A couple of metal window shades rolled up like garage doors, seemingly activated by the opening of the door. With the light, Tzaro could see all seats had been removed but two, flat screens mounted on their backs. Quill's kitchen was a fold-out steel sink, a hot plate, and a microwave that looked salvaged. His mini-refrigerator magnet read *Planet of the Apps*.

"So cool!" Svetla gushed.

"Very," Tzaro added. Wilson ducked under the web of wiring in the ceiling.

"I was totally bummed when the group moved from Alameda into the city, but the rent is like nothing and I can basically do anything I want with it."

Quill pulled a drawer of a red metal tool chest and extracted a lock fob from between pairs of jeans.

"Okay," he said, "to Bernal."

Bernal Heights was on the way back toward the skyline Tzaro had seen from the Bay Bridge. Stucco bungalows in candy wafer colors crowded together on twisty hills. Quill and Morgan zoomed into a drive of a pale pink "For Sale" model and Svetla rolled to a stop behind them. Quill beat a path around the back of the house and Morgan hustled after him.

"It isn't really for sale," he said at the back door as the others filled in. "It is and it isn't.

"My mom owns it. Our friends, and geekers like me, stay here, freedom fighters ... I wish we'd had this in Babi Ganoush," he directed toward Morgan. Tzaro picked up on the battle versus Alibaba for low-rent zones in Oakland. Quill presented the fob to the lock and it clicked.

They entered a kitchen, small by current standards, curiously accented by a black refrigerator and range and dark counters from the slab-granite era.

"There's beer here. A lot of beer." He grinned in the light from the refrigerator that appeared to showcase a dozen microbreweries. "And there's a freezer of food in the basement. That's the thing, okay, no deliveries? We need to keep it a safe house. There's a bike in the garage for local travel, same as mine."

Quill led them into the living room, warm in the dark with all the blinds closed. The spare furniture looked like a realtor's staging. Tzaro could think only of the beer and whatever was in the freezer. His stomach was churning.

"Air mattress under the sofa right there, and three bedrooms upstairs. Please leave the blinds pulled. Just remember, you aren't here. And if you could park on the street, a little up the block," he said to Svetla. "Thanks."

"Hey," Morgan said, "thank *you*."

"So." Quill reset the conversation. "Morgan tells me you're here for a reason."

"We're trying to find out—" Tzaro started.

"About the exploit," Quill completed. "Right, got it. I can tell you this—we've lost some people. Nobody's on top of it yet."

"Pardon, excuse me," Carmody cut in looking tired, but he was on his message. "I think our technical specialist is best suited to summarize. Wesley?"

Wes's eyes came on and he drew himself up. His window had been clicked to the front. "I'd be interested to talk to any of your colleagues who are into protocols. Especially anyone who may have some PUD-Z."

"That would be Natalie. She's so eloquent, gold code, DRY to the max. Her dad like created THP."

"Jerry Roberts?"

"Yes!" Quill brightened, clearly delighted, gave Wes an elbow bump. "She'll be in the store tomorrow before club time, around six."

After they repeated their thanks, Morgan followed Quill outside to his bike, and Svetla left to move her car down the block. Carmody and Wilson went to explore the rooms upstairs.

Tzaro pulled a Hop City from the door of cold blue light. Among all the beers, he was glad to see the one that connected back. He had half the IPA down by the time he closed the door.

Derek was close, he knew. A two-hour flight. Therica was about equidistant. He swigged the rest. Their futures were in his hands.

He pulled another, a Rogue Dead Guy Ale, and headed toward the stairs. The next evening, he was thinking, the earliest to get Wes with Natalie.

In the staircase window the sun stopped him, a fiery half dome over the Pacific. Every minute, he thought, all of the few minutes they had combusting away. He topped the stairs and headed for the shower, content to let the freezer wait for a few more minutes. He envisioned mic'ed Mexican, or lasagna.

He had emptied the second by the time he stood under the warm rain of the shower head. With nothing to cling to but the arrogance of faith, he let the minutes go their way. Eventually they started to reclaim as much of their promise as their loss.

Ripping the tape gun over box tops, tearing lengths to seal the sides. Stacks of boxes in her Rogers Park apartment, the summer sublet after Evanston. Dark old doors and wainscoting, high ceilings, maximum gothic. Green Leinenkugel's bottles, daisies in her carafe looking downcast. All temporary. She and a roommate with a lease already signed on a two-bedroom basement in Harlem, a four-block walk from Columbia.

Wearing her Northwestern sweatshirt and jeans? T and shorts? At the end of August, Chicago still humid and hot. Making love in all of that, at some point between packing her books and her pans? Odds close to absolute they did, sweet inevitability of the time.

Smart-mouthing and cutting up, no doubt. How could it have been, both of them packing her for New

York and he, pending a simple college acceptance, bound for the other coast?

Of course he would see her soon, a few hours from O'Hare to JFK. No plan for it then, not what they did. Seeing her only once more was unimaginable. In the days to come, predictably but somehow incredibly, as though he was living out a dream, realities of school and career and then marriage intervening.

But to them in their world in those days, realities were useless.

CHAPTER 19   STRANGE DAYS

Tzaro was in a strange city. Although strange, it was not unknown to him. He had been there before in what seemed like a previous lifetime. Also familiar—he was trying to get back to her. She could have reached the airport already. If he could grab a taxi, he had a chance to catch her in the terminal before her gate. But his clothes and suitcase were still in the room and it was twelve minutes to checkout time. He could call or text the hotel, but his phone was somewhere on the island.

A tread woke him. A bolt of adrenaline. Business shoes, hard steps, parallel to his head on the air mattress in front of the living room sofa. All the others were upstairs.

Slices of light lined the blinds, filtered not bright. He flashed on the scene in Moran Park. What they were doing was not benign, and Quill must have his enemies too.

He checked the front door, same as the night before: solid wood with deadbolt, as though that mattered much. He reviewed his exits—to the stairs and the kitchen—then lay perfectly still, chest pounding. He tried to detect whispers.

The shoes were on the move, shuffling along the porch toward the window. Whoever it was would try to glimpse around the blinds.

Abruptly the shoes returned, halted before the door. Tzaro fought the vision of the lock imploding, the frame splintering from a boot in the middle of the thin wooden panel. Instead he focused on Wilson's room, second in the hall. He would be the strongest ally. Tzaro gathered himself for a break to the stairs.

Two more heavy steps before the door, then silence. Tzaro's senses were recalibrating, reverting to prehuman clarity. He tuned to any creak, any contusions of microfibers. The seconds dragged. Attenuated seconds, time stretched thin. Silence stretched to a single fiber.

At the end of the fiber, he drew his legs up slowly and rolled to his knees. One foot forward, hands on thighs, he pushed himself up by inches until he stood, light-headed and wavering. When he was steady, he tiptoed to the window and settled his ear close to the blind. Nothing. With his face back from the window, he lifted the edge of the slats.

Except for the staged rocking chair, the front porch was empty. On the street in front of the house next door, Tzaro spotted a lime green Assage hybrid. A plus-size redhead in a too-short skirt rounded the back and slipped into the driver seat and the chassis bounced. As it pulled away, Tzaro waited in his undershorts, downshifting, his pulse starting to normalize.

Finally he opened the lock and pulled the door ajar. A tiny face smiled up from the threshold. He reached for the card.

Katie Mondaine of House and Home Realty popped from her rectangle in 3-D, broad shouldered, formidable. In the kitchen he spotted a recycle bin, and as he dropped it in, he noticed it had company—at least half a dozen other hopefuls.

"You're up too," Svetla said from the kitchen. She seemed like too much too fast. His head was muddled with struggles, still trying to process the straight drop from the dream into the heart-tripping sales call. She looked smaller in her nightshirt, spindly legs. "There was somebody out there, right? I can hear things like that. They say I'm hypersensitive."

"It was a realtor. I thought we were being cased—checked out for a break-in."

"Or somebody stalking Morgan. That girl's been into some shit. So you slept down here. Good call. It's hot as Hayleys up there. So now that we're up ..." She went to the fridge and pulled the door.

"Is there cereal somewhere, or just beer?" She started on the cabinets. "Do you think we'll be stuck in this jailhouse all day?"

They would need to get through to evening to try Natalie at the club. As they settled in, morning dragged toward afternoon, and the jailhouse metaphor seemed more apt by the hour.

Morgan climbed the stairs two at a time to stay tuned, slid on the banister, and hung from the spindles. Wilson found three wiffle balls in the basement, and he and the professor and Tzaro pitched and drop-kicked in the upstairs hall.

Downstairs Svetla danced to music from Morgan's phone, then paced the house and eventually retreated to the bathroom with nail polish. Wes began on R.B., researching all variants of UPD, but by noon he was pacing too.

Tzaro tried to focus off the time. He was immobilized in a prison of his own making. Therica seemed farther away by the minute. He envisioned Derek in math camp, now in favor of anything that kept him off his phone.

By the time the morning fog cleared, bright light edged the blinds and shades. Their one fan simply recirculated the heat. By early afternoon they were all in a state of torpor down-stairs.

"I can't stand this!" Bolting up from the sofa, Svetla said it for them all. "Here we are in the big City by the Bay, right? I for one have never seen it. Let's go on a tour. My treat." She pranced over to Morgan and tweaked her cheek. "You will be our guide, won't you, Sweetie. You get to tell me where to go and what to do, and I know you like that."

"So now I'm supposed to be a freaking tour guide. Seriously?"

"She does have a point, my dear," Carmody said. "We're pretty much stymied until this evening. And Wes and I probably remember enough to spell you with your docent duties."

"I could use coffee," Wilson said. "Triple tall cappuccino." Tzaro just stared at him.

"What do you say, Wesley?"

He folded the laptop under his arm.

"Let's start with the Fillmore," he said. "We'll work up the hill from there."

They did start with Fillmore, but for Tzaro and the others, it could have been anywhere. Just escaping the house in Bernal brought a huge charge of freedom. With high nostalgia Calvin and Wes pointed to the site of the former Bill Graham's Fillmore. They filled up on coffee, including Wilson's triple, then headed north, Gough to Franklin at the edge of Pacific Heights: apartments with bay windows on climbing and pitching blocks. Breeze from the bay channeled up through the streets. Vivid colors, every new view a photo. Tzaro got it for the first time—the San Francisco intoxication, irresistible. But as they climbed toward Telegraph Hill, he saw something the others missed. The Hayes Street cable car rattled by in high tourist season with the conductor and two riders. He flashed on the Portland trolley.

On the other side of Hayes, a Chinese old-timer in baggy pants was sitting on the step of an apartment building. Their eyes met for a moment. The man scrambled up and disappeared inside the door.

In North Beach the sunlight was unnaturally bright. The intersection of Broadway and Columbus was howling with sirens. Across the alley from City Lights Bookstore, Café Vesuvio was dark.

"Did you see that?" Carmody asked.

"I've never seen that," Wes replied.

"The city," the professor said, "it's not the same."

"No," Tzaro said absently. "It wouldn't be."

The time had come to find Natalie. They headed for south of Market.

"She's not here yet," Quill told them. "If you guys would like to chill."

Gasoline Valley was morphing toward its true self. The napalm hills glowed with backlight, and around the walls, table lighting cycled nearly imperceptibly from orange to green. They took a booth.

Tzaro spotted Quill's colleague from the day before in the Megadeth booth, staring into the murky glow of his screen. Stick figures, half a dozen or so Giacomettis, were drifting on the floor, dark clothes, sallow and haunted looking.

"The Angels are out," Quill said. "They're not stoned, it's like their kind of meditation. Then later they do these awesome dances." He had adopted an evening look too. His long black hair was cinched in a ponytail, and Tzaro detected eyeshade and mascara.

"You guys eat? No? They have killer souvlaki. It's vegan." Quill's hip purred and he took the call.

"Scusie," he said and left to join his partner in the Megadeth booth.

"Is that the security biz," Svetla said to Morgan, "or something?"

The euphemism for marginal was obvious—the hacker persona. Morgan seemed to be struggling with saying the obvious. She was rescued by the appearance of a waitress at their table.

"My name is Nyx. Can I get you guys something?" She spoke with a slight accent like a recorded greeting. Eyes bright and with lips pleasantly pursed, she wore a black leotard and tights, Balanchine era. Perfect posture.

"A holo," Tzaro heard Morgan whisper to Wes. He betrayed a hint of a grin.

"Do you have souvlaki?" he asked.

"We have souvlaki," Nyx confirmed. "It is vegan." Tzaro admired the hologram, physically perfect but literally empty. Her eyes reminded him of *Blue Moon*.

"I'll have one, and your Red Hook on draft," Wes said. "Put my friends' orders on my bill. I'm just curious about this place. Could you tell me how many people are here right now, in this building?"

"Twenty-one. You three, the hostess, ten on the floor, four in the booths, two behind the stage. And Nyx."

"Thank you. And what are our lat-long coordinates?"

"Latitude 37.77, longitude -122.41."

"Interesting. Thank you. And one more thing—for my order, please hold the onion." Nyx took the other orders and disappeared, Wes grinned until she returned directly. She stood looking to him for approval, holding an onion.

"Thank you," he said and she retreated.

"One for the humans," he said, looking delighted.

As they were finishing, music began from a sound system, electric pop mixed with what sounded like chopper blades and a didgeridoo. The Angels were beginning to bop, gyros with outstretched arms, two colliding and spinning off into open floor, then bouncing like pogo sticks.

Others began to filter in. Tzaro noted them, spike-haired, pinned, and inked, although he would rather not. He was hoping for Natalie, as though she would be holding a sign. Quill was long gone, vanished with his security hacker accomplice, Tzaro guessed, into the nether regions behind the stage.

Wilson had gone outside, unable to tolerate the music. Svetla had dragged Morgan to the floor. Carmody, Wes, and Tzaro remained at the table.

Tzaro inspected his plate. It revealed nothing. The day had been endless, and their long-awaited luminary, another kid no doubt, and a hacker herself, was likely a no-show. He was sick of the day and night and his second warm beer. He leaned across the table to Wes to try to be heard.

"What do we have on this, right now, just ourselves?"

"Right now I'm saying it's PUD-Z. Ninety percent confidence. We know about Novosibirsk—Siberia. There might be another group here somewhere. But anyone or anything with the means to buy talent... given the scale, we should expect financial coordination, payment laundering, a lot of firepower."

Tzaro felt the weight of the assessment dragging him down.

"So, burial or cremation?" Wes was forcing a grin.

Tzaro read the veteran coder's face, and Carmody's. He had dragged them into a no-win. Going farther down the same road was becoming farther from the reason he had come. It was time to fold. He stared into his plate like one more mandala, clearing his mind to find the words. He became aware of a presence at the table that wasn't Nyx.

"Quill said to meet you here. I'm Natalie."

CHAPTER 20   DARK NIGHT

Natalie was wearing a man's short-sleeved shirt in a light summer plaid over jeans with sandals. Close-cropped platinum hair with purple highlights and pale blue eyes gave her a Jimmy Buffett beach girl granddaughter's look.

Tzaro made their introductions and caught himself before asking how she found them, realizing they couldn't look more obviously out of place.

"We're hoping for your help with a computer thing. Quill told us you're an expert in network protocols. Wes is—"

"You're trying to crack the Wundrus exploit. You're not alone. Let's talk."

Natalie motioned with her head and they followed her past night creatures who had made it through security. Just before the front door she diverged to an anteroom and pulled the steel door. They entered a functional concrete bunker with a metal folding table and chairs, easy breakdown furnishings for a band of hacker nomads. *Altered* and *Chain of Nails* posters adorned the walls.

"What's your take?" Natalie reversed a chair and straddled it. Wes took a spot two chairs away.

"It's persistent. They're using a no-authentication protocol, basically logging in anonymous. It's a really early piece of the backbone—UDP—but its latest incarnation."

"PUD-Z."

Wes lit up. He unfolded R.B. and Natalie slid closer

"Quill told me your dad is Jerry Roberts. That explains a lot. We're contemporaries, as they say, a.k.a. old coders."

"And you wrote *QuetzalCalc*. Hey, we know who Wes Englehart is."

Tzaro recognized intimacy of the kind to which neither he nor the professor had access. He nodded toward the door. Soon he and Carmody were outside on the south of Market sidewalk in the useless grandeur of the August night.

"An excellent decision, I quite agree." Carmody hit his usual stride.

"I hope Wes can connect the dots." Despite the glint of hope Natalie provided, Tzaro couldn't shake the sense that he was responsible for opening a door to nowhere. Even if they could locate the source, they would be outclassed and outgunned.

"If anyone can," Carmody said.

They strode on as though they had a destination. An articulated bus rolled by, one sallow rider under fluorescents. A siren wailed somewhere on the city side of Market Street.

> Standing room only, packed on the MTA train. Front-to-front, how lucky could he be, not just then but all-time, all the time they were together. Rattling old car lurching and sighing on the rails. She in her dark navy peacoat pressed against him.
>
> Winter a dismal time to be in Boston, just when they could. A higher irony to be in that old hotel, the Buckminster, a two-minute walk to Fenway Park. On any reasonable summer day he would be working scalpers for tickets. Instead, the hike from the station

to the hotel in the cold, or more like the idea of the cold, the must-be cold, floating as they were inches above the ground.

Climbing the old stairs in front of him, her strides almost as long as his. Unlocking, then closing the door thick as an old table behind them, dark shellac, brass knob, locking. The enveloping heat, brass bed, heavy curtains a shelter for decades of lovers. Finally free to strip, skin-to-skin, the lingering scent of cold in her hair.

"You're experiencing a crisis of faith," Carmody stated, not asked.

Beyond his erudition, it was that kind of sixth sense that made his reputation with students. He touched Tzaro's arm but only for a moment.

"Dark night of the soul," he said as though he had simply recognized a symptom or read a street sign. "Originally a poem, St. John of the Cross, sixteenth century. We've all been there.

"My earliest, and certainly darkest at the time, was right here, Svetla's City by the Bay. I was in my sixth year at the University of San Francisco and had applied for tenure. Unfortunately, I was also in something of a war.

"The issue was early Chomsky—generative grammar. I argued not only was it syntonic with pictographic vocabularies, it was central to the syntax. The proof was set theory. At the time Sociology ruled, same at Berkeley, and not just here. Sets were irrelevant because language was a product of cultural dynamics, you see. Aside from being an absurdity, the argument was solipsistic, took its conclusion as its premise. Basically, the head of the department, Miranda Lunes was her name—and apt it was, I thought—didn't understand sets and lacked the enthusiasm to learn. We had a skirmish or two on the faculty level, and a public debate for the entertainment of our students. I accomplished something of a draw in the opinion of the audience, which I took as a victory, given the preponderance of Sociology types."

Tzaro imagined it was after the days of Wes and the Catacombs. He thought about asking the year, but Carmody was on a roll.

"In deference to Pyrrhus, my victory was short-lived. As you've no doubt guessed, my tenure was denied. But what may surprise you, as it flabbergasted me at the time—I was released. Dismissed from my position."

Tzaro fell a half-stride behind. He was thinking suddenly of sitting with Lauren at the dining table with Cal and Tipi. And meetings later. He never imagined the professor had once been canned.

"There was empty rhetoric about a reorg, priorities, a five-year plan, and so on. Obfuscations. It was a vendetta, pure and simple. And ... as the fates conspired, Claire was just starting at Pomona and Tipi's associate's hours had been reduced." At the end of the block, they crossed to the opposite side against the light, the street empty of traffic.

"But miraculously, we survived—in hindsight, to some extent prevailed. Your alma mater has been astute in its judgment and if somewhat short of generous, at least consistent, not whimsical.

"The point of this self-disclosure is that over the course of the dark night, with its trials and reversals, I had to hang in. Quitting was not an option. And now, as you well know, generative is the prevailing thesis. I wasn't always confident that I was right. When I was approached to debate Miranda Lunes, I considered refusing, going with the flow. But the forces that were in motion had to play out.

"Right or wrong, you must acknowledge the forces you've set in motion. You must find out."

They took the rest of the block in silence. An occasional hiss of tires. By the time they reached the intersection, Tzaro saw the green light and the white Walk icon differently.

"Hey," he called from the middle of the street. Two-thirds down the block, the big man looked back then waited until they caught up.

"Welcome to Injun territory." Wilson looked refreshed.

"We need to get back." Tzaro took up Carmody's pace, and Wilson and the professor fell in. "Wes has it all now, I can feel it."

CHAPTER 21   NYXED

"This is a membership club." The brick-head in the doorway had Tzaro by half a foot in height and almost a foot on either side. His cologne was acting like ipecac.

"We were just here—we left to get some air."

Brick-head was impassive. Tzaro tried to focus off the lead-colored half of his left eye, which, on some battleground of his fetid youth, could have been poked by a sharp stick.

"You got a card? I haven't seen you."

"Excuse me," the professor put in, "Quill is our host. If he's available—"

"A lot of people know Quill," the brick-head countered.

"One of our party is inside talking to Natalie. You can—"

"Quill said to give you this." Wilson cut in between them. His hand almost covered the square Ziploc.

Brick-head took it and straightened. He and Wilson were eye-to-eye. An oyster-sized muscle slid in his jaw.

"Snohomish red," Wilson said.

The head tilted back a degree, the eyes narrowed, and Tzaro saw the bag disappear, sleight of hand, into brick-head's jacket pocket. He looked to the next in line, a couple of waifs, and nodded them all in.

The anteroom was empty. The only alternative was the dark, reverberating hollow of the club. During their time outside, the music had morphed into bass-heavy techno funk.

They stepped in, trying to spot Wes. A heady smell of weed and hash smokes met them, and a covering scent like frankincense. Under it all was more than a hint of chlorine. A mop and bleach, Tzaro thought. Someone had thrown up.

At the end of the room the napalm hills were livid, pulsing yellow and orange. Between Tzaro and the stage, the floor was hopping with black cutouts. A female animal crossed in front of him—her black tube top festooned with replica barbed wire. Her black bikini bottom also. On her butt in white: Prop of Rubio.

"Great," Tzaro thought he heard dimly over the music an instant before he realized the message was directed at him from a few feet away. "She was great."

"Hey! We didn't know where—"

"What?" Wes cupped his ear.

"Never mind. Natalie, you mean?" Tzaro shouted. "It was good?"

Carmody ushered them to the side wall, out of the fray.

"She said PUD-Z is easy to intercept," Wes went on. "It's cloaked in an FTP account and pushed from a series of IP's—that's to be expected. But she has code that can rewind—using any of the server log files, she can trace back to the originating servers. I have a couple of the logs already from servers close to Wundrus—don't ask, don't tell. She's sending me the code. It has to be from her machine through an encrypted tunnel. I'll install when we get out of here. Jesus."

Tzaro looked where Wes was looking and caught most of it. In front of the stage backlit by napalm, an Angel had been tossed above the bouncing heads and came down like a rag doll. The tribe swallowed him up.

"Have you seen the ladies?" Tzaro shouted back.

Wes shook his head.

Wilson was pointing into the room.

Among the dancers but not dancing, Svetla was darting through the crowd with quick glances like an anxious bird. Tzaro waved with one arm and then two until she spotted him.

"Have you seen Morgan?" she shouted as soon as she was within earshot, short of breath. Her upper lip glistened. "I went to the bathroom and then I couldn't find her." She looked back furtively across the floor.

"Maybe she's with Quill," Carmody ventured. "Have you seen him?"

She barely responded, but it was a no.

Tzaro was feeling dizzy and tired of tracking juveniles like a camp counselor.

"I sent it to you." Natalie had materialized while Tzaro was focused on their lost sheep.

"Great, that's great, thanks." Wes beamed. "I want to install, but it seems we've lost track of one of our group. I need to—one moment, please."

"Excuse me, miss?"

Tzaro wondered what he was doing.

"My name is Nyx. Can I get you something?"

"Nyx, do you know who Quill is?" She took one dispassionate second.

"I know who Quill is."

"Can you tell me where he is?"

Her holographic projection and persona took more than a second. Several seconds.

"Quill is not here. Follow me, please." She turned and began striding purposefully, head up, posture perfect. Tzaro realized she was heading for the door.

Wes shot them all a glance, clearly pleased with himself. They followed, past the brick-head and out into the night. Nyx was moving briskly. They hung a right at the alley and followed her behind the club.

"Quill parks his motorcycle here." They surveyed the first of the four incursion-proof xynostyrene cubicles, the rest occupied with bikes.

"Because Quill is not inside the Gasoline Valley club, and because his motorcycle is not in his parking pod, Quill is gone."

"Thank you," Wes said. Her blue holographic irises met his. "Can you tell us where he's gone?"

Nyx looked away, down the alley in the direction of the city. Seconds passed.

Wes knew the search was likely off into genealogical and psychological profile databases, cross-referencing interactions with web viewing preferences, public recordings, and private billing records. An endless half-minute passed. No hits.

"He doesn't pick up," Natalie said, lowering her phone. "No surprise. He could be tracked."

"Do you have any idea where he could be?" Tzaro saw her clutch for an instant.

"If you have any—" Svetla started.

"He could be with someone," Wilson put in. "Dangerous for both of them."

"Look, I don't ..." Natalie was shaking her head, looking away.

Tzaro got it. In their world, unless you're sure what's up, you say nothing.

"Listen," Svetla shot, "we have a missing person here. We're thinking kidnapping. As in federal, you're hearing me? We can check his bus, okay? But if he's not there and we have to call police—"

"Quill said you were in the Bernal house," Natalie began, forcing the words. "His mom has another place in the East Bay, Oakland. He bought it for her after one of our big jobs, shall remain nameless. Paid cash. It was a foreclosure. She lives there but it's been a safe house too. It's a good place to get lost.

"Here," she said to Wes, tapping a series on her phone. "Address is in your box."

"All right?" she threw back at Svetla as though she needed a Cochlear Cadet. "All right."

"One thing," she went on, "when you go there, don't be dumb. Too smart either." Natalie started back down the alley.

"Thank you," Wes called after her, "for everything."

She raised one hand but kept going.

"Let's go to Oakland." Svetla was already walking her bird walk, picking up speed. Wilson and Carmody followed.

Nyx was still processing.

"Thank you," Wes said, "that's all we need."

She woke from her reverie, smiled politely, and started in.

Tzaro looked at Wes.

"No," Wes confirmed before he was asked, "you don't tip a hologram."

CHAPTER 22   SPEAR SIX

"Quill, don't shoot!" Tzaro shouted from behind the fender toward the house. He and Wilson were hunkering behind the car for cover. The others were still inside, hunched below the windows. Wilson had spotted it first, surreal but unmistakable: a barrel—hunting rifle—protruding between blinds from a second-story window.

"They're cool, they're cool!" a male voice came from inside.

Tzaro peered over the hood just enough to see the barrel retract. After a long minute the front door of the little stucco fortress opened and Quill waved them in.

"It's my mom," he said sheepishly, "she's very protective." Morgan appeared beside him and was immediately squeezed by Svetla and shoulder pounded by the others with great relief. They had sped from the club to the junkyard and found no one in Quill's bus.

"What are you doing?" Svetla started in on him. "Why is she here? This is like kidnapping—"

"He saw somebody." Morgan stopped her.

"He was stalking her," Quill said. "We had to split ASAP. You don't screw around with this guy."

"What guy? Why?"

"Cheung. He goes back. He's a corporate assassin hired to neutralize certain non-corporate activist types. He's very good at his job. Morgan and I got hip to him back in the Google-Tenderloin days. He slimed into the club with a fake card and disguised—hair color and makeup."

"So how did you know who he was?" Svetla shifted from indignant to curious.

"He has a thing with his left foot. It doesn't lift right when he walks. He couldn't hide that."

"I was going to call you from his mom's landline," Morgan explained, "but we didn't know what he could hook. We're super-hot right now, so if he could intercept, he could track back to you."

"What's next? She's safe here." Quill's own protective wing was showing.

"Not sure," Tzaro said. "Natalie gave Wes a lot—"

"You were right," Wes picked up. "She nails her protocols. And she gave me a log tracer. It's supposed to track an FTP push back to its origin server. You probably know—"

"Spear Six? Have you installed it? Come on."

They followed Quill into his mom's house, and Tzaro took in the high points of the living room. A green La-Z-Boy recliner and sofa with throw pillows, fringed. Porcelain bric-a-brac on an end table. A dominant print of a gnarled tree with pink blooms in a gilt frame.

Quill pulled out a chair for Wes at the dining table under a glass chandelier with candle flame bulbs. They all clumped around his screen.

"Install Spear Six," he said, and the installation completed in seconds.

"Can you get a log file?" Quill asked.

"I have two. A dark diver I know helped me out. This one is from a Wundrus mirror, supposed to be one of the first. I could pre-parse it…"

"Like picking fly shit out of pepper," Quill said. "Not worth it."

Spear Six was a command line utility with a block cursor, an interface after Wes's own heart. He pressed F1 for help and the text commands and arguments rolled up the screen.

"It's *trace*," Quill confirmed.

Wes typed it, followed by the path to the log file, and pressed Enter.

The screen refilled with text scrolling at an unreadable speed, followed in a few seconds by a prompt: *Save location and show.*

"Okay," Wes said. The file saved and a terrain view filled the screen, a lightly limned circle floating over woodland. Wes tapped a key to zoom out. They all tightened around him and peered into the screen.

At the right distance, the woods took on the contours of hills with scattered clumps of dots like rooftops. A band of highway edged into the right side of the screen, to the east.

The circle hovered over a dark patch of hills between settlements. As Wes moved the pointer inside the circle, coordinates appeared beside it, and name labels. He moved it to the center.

Gold numbers stacked beside the pointer: 37.09 N, 122.09 W. Below the lat-long, the name.

"Holy shit, it's Ben Lomond!" Morgan checked Carmody and Wes, the Bay Area expats. They shook their heads.

"It's in the Santa Cruz Mountains, down 101 around Boulder Creek and Felton. I've camped all around there."

"To clarify for myself," Carmody began, "this program is indicating that the source of the FTP transmissions, which cloak the PUD-Z transmissions—both of which have been infecting the largest social networking sites in the world with terrible consequences—is in the woods in the hills above Santa Cruz."

Wes peered up over his glasses at his former romantic rival and buddy. "It's the best we have."

Svetla left little time for rumination. "Like *all* that you have, more like it."

They were suddenly silent as the situation sank in. Tzaro felt cut loose, rootless and groundless. The way the professor had put it, the absurdity of it, had his head spinning with doubts. In the face of absurdity, how to act?

Wes started to laugh. A half-chuckle and a grin.

Carmody took it up. Then he burst into laughter, slapping palms onto thighs. In that moment Tzaro saw who he was—the laughing Buddha, irresistible.

"I think Sparky likes it," Wilson said, and then they were all laughing. All but Quill.

"So what are you going to do? This could be a bot farm, nobody there but drone strikes to take you out. These are bad people. You need badder. They're the antichrist, I know, but the FBI—"

"It's where we started," Tzaro said. "They…disbelieve."

"We're insane to everyone but ourselves," Carmody clarified.

Quill forced a grin.

"Your perspective is appreciated by your humble servant. But what I'm asking is, what are you going to *do*? You can all be, how shall I say, fucking annihilated."

"That kind of language isn't necessary in this house."

"Sorry," said the son.

Quill's mother had materialized in the hall behind them, short and stocky in a heat-beater Mumu spattered with hibiscus. Tzaro reset his assumptions about Quill from east Asian to Hawaiian, at least half. The leather strap of a .30-30 Winchester graced her shoulder.

"You are welcome to stay the night." Her expression of reprimand modulated into a Sweet 'n Low smile.

Silence followed. Tzaro could see they lacked the will to go on.

"Thank you, but we are leaving tonight." All eyes went to Svetla.

"We have no time to spend now. Do we?" She pointed her message at all around the table, clearly impatient with the hesitant. "How long, Morgan?"

"An hour and a half from the city, maybe less from the East Bay."

She turned back to their hostess. "Thank you for your hospital. We must go now."

Inviting no further input, she pivoted and in a moment was out the door and into the night.

They glanced at one another. Wilson shrugged. The professor laughed again and followed, and the rest fell in behind him.

"Hang on two seconds. I want to go with you." Tzaro was close enough to hear Quill entreating Morgan.

"No way, I'll be fine. This is my thing. Besides, there's no room in the car."

"Take this," he said, and Tzaro saw the silver glint of a pistol as he stuffed it into her backpack. "You could really get foo'ed here. Don't underestimate, especially Cheung."

"Hey thanks," she said, giving him a quick hug. "I'll call."

As Tzaro crossed the yard to the car, the sky seemed lower, marbled with clouds. The warm night weighed on him, retarding his purpose. It seemed to say, settle, let larger forces have their way. But they could be a few hours from knowing. Right or wrong, he had set the forces in motion, his professor the Buddha had observed. Consequently, they were all crossing a line where turning back would no longer be an option.

"There is one more month left from the summer." Svetla called over her shoulder. And then as she pulled her door, "I cannot spend until Halloween on this road trip carnival. Morgan, honey, which way do I go?"

They were taking their positions in the car, Tzaro waiting for Wes to climb in before him, when he felt the bump, too familiar. He glanced at the others, hoping he was the only one who noticed, as though confirmation was required to give his fear true form. But already, he knew what he knew—he was paid to. And in the next moment, confirmation became unnecessary.

CHAPTER 23   OCCURRENCE AT HAWK CREEK

Tzaro was the only one left outside the car. Bump again, quickly another, in his shoes. S-wave or P? The slip, he thought, how close? How near to vertical?

Svetla's voice first from the car, high-pitched—"What?" or a sound not quite a word.

Tzaro's eye went to the closest light pole—oscillation, clear as a flag, undeniable P-waves. He ducked in and pulled the door.

"Is this—" Wes started.

"Earthquake!" Morgan finished.

"We're good," Tzaro said. "This is the safest place."

Svetla had already started the car. It began to sway.

She screamed something in Bulgarian. Wilson's hand went to her shoulder.

The streetlight rocked into sudden dark. The street in front of them looked shockingly severe in the headlights.

"Quill," Morgan said and they all checked the house. It was still light, a patch of window light on the lawn.

A horn began to blast somewhere behind them, a mindless pulse. Car alarm.

Thoughts flooded Tzaro's brain in burst mode, data overload, panic thoughts mixed with recall. Severity? MMS over latest months, max in the low fives, was it off Monterey? Last worst? Loma Prieta, the Bay Bridge opening like a trap door. Odds of a remote trigger in Pasadena? Was it only a foreshock?

"Svetla, let's go," he heard himself command.

"Let me check Quill." Morgan's hand was on the door handle.

"Can't! Listen, they're okay. We could be trapped here in minutes. Svetla!" Tzaro shouted, a blast of urgency she was powerless to resist.

She gunned into a U-turn, and the Grand Marquis lurched sideways then plunged forward. Morgan's door swung open on the turn but slammed shut as the big car righted itself.

"I'm calling," she said defiantly.

"Quill's phone is not on, we were told," Carmody recalled.

"Damn! No service."

"Jammed," Tzaro said. "It will be. But we need GPS."

Svetla was hurtling down dark blocks, street signs passing as shadowy blurs. It was clear Tzaro was right.

"Okay, okay, keep going here. We'll need to take Eighteenth to Market." Morgan peered into the beam from her hand and fingered the app. "In two blocks hang a right."

"What are the options?" Wes asked. He had R.B. open on a map.

"The Bay Bridge. Maybe not ideal, right?" She let it lay, the implication that they could be swinging on the long bridge high over open water being clear enough. "Much closer, the Nimitz—880."

The Loma Prieta highway disaster. Fifteen seconds of shock and roll sent the overpass imploding into rubble, flattening a block of cars. Thirty dead, or forty? Tzaro didn't know who in their party would recall it. Cal would, and probably Wes. Tzaro kept quiet.

Svetla turned, and they ascended a light grade. Two other sets of headlights appeared, cruising sharklike through intersections of dead traffic signals. Half of the block ahead of them was slick, an open hydrant somewhere, or a breached water main.

A siren blasted suddenly behind them and then it was on them.

"Fuck!" Svetla lurched toward the curb and they bounced halfway onto the sidewalk. A burst of red light lit up the car, and then the howling was past them. She shot off a volley of Bulgarian curses, took a breath, and then backed onto the asphalt.

"Jesus." Morgan had retrieved her phone from the floor and was recalibrating.

"Next is Market, am I right?" Wes had kept them in sight on R.B.

"Yeah, right on Market—one block."

They were hearing more sirens. Svetla turned and they rolled on in silence. At the next intersection a black man in shorts and T-shirt was shining a flashlight, holding the car in the cross-street, waving Svetla through.

"Extraordinary," the professor remarked. "A citizen."

A firefighter? Tzaro wondered. Or a citizen extraordinary brought to life in the moment.

Another left, on Seventh.

"There it is." Morgan identified the distant regular procession of lights as the Nimitz Freeway. Relief was palpable in the car. They were in sight of others who were moving purposefully, and safely.

Tzaro checked the streets they crossed, and as much of Oakland as he could see. A pile of bricks spilled over the sidewalk in the middle of a block. He was mainly looking for fire, seeing no sign. Soon they closed within a few blocks of the freeway.

"There will be a ramp?" Svetla asked Morgan who was peering around her seat back.

"Right, on Broadway—"

"Look out!" Wilson had an open line of sight over an empty lot, and he saw it first as they approached a cross-street.

The semi cab was not stopping. It bore down on the intersection steadily, roof alive with sparks, a rolling hallucination.

"Stop!" It could have been Morgan shouting, but it was all of them.

They were on a dead collision course.

Svetla braked and Tzaro pitched forward into his shoulder belt. The brakes grabbed and the car fish-tailed and died.

The cab flashed hugely in front of them, top sparking, and plowed through the intersection.

They sat in the stalled car, gasping.

The driverless semi, chunk of transformer on the roof and a metal pole dragging behind, sparked down the street. A block or so distant, they heard a crash, and a burst of white illuminated the dark.

"How could that..." Morgan couldn't finish.

"Kick-started, I'd say," Wes ventured. "The transformer must have arced and started it when the pole came down."

"You see autonomous," Svetla fumed. "I'll take the humans, okay? However nuts. They know how to stop. Most of them."

A long moment passed. The smell of the hot engine mixed with burned rubber. Eventually Svetla rotated the key. Sputters.

She stopped, rotated again. The engine caught. She shifted, and in a moment they were rolling slowly, straightening out. Then they were under the highway and onto the on-ramp.

Tzaro waited until they had joined the steady, companionable flow of headlights heading south.

"Wes, could you pull up USGS for me?"

Tzaro scanned the face of R.B. MMS 5.4, epicenter between Pacifica and San Mateo. Two beads he recalled, on the necklace of the San Andreas. No fatalities reported yet, no trigger events.

He scanned right, over the bay toward San Francisco. Distant sirens but no visible spots of fire.

"How did I do this?" Svetla was shaking her head. "We get back, I'm charging double. There will be a CV boot replace, I know it, I've been through that one. Get ready to pay double."

They were over an hour out of Oakland. They had been rolling through the dark, saying little, recovering. Tzaro gazed out the opposite window, not seeing the traffic. He was far away. Somehow Morgan, from her seat by the window, could tell where. She held up her phone.

"Your kid?" she said.

He spun for a second, mind-read, feeling naked. Was he that obvious?

"Thanks, but I think it would be late for him." Before he could block the thought, he wondered if he should grab the chance, if it could be his last call with Derek. And if Morgan was thinking that too. "Thanks, though," he said again. "Thank you."

Morgan half-nodded and slipped her Galaxy into her thigh pocket.

Tzaro tried to focus on the Spear Six ring on Wes's screen, the color turning from white to green as they got closer. He became aware of the tightness in his shoulders and tried to roll it out. Over the drive his muscles had been clenching by degrees. He picked it up from the others too, the tension building in all of them like a shared force. He checked the time: ten thirty-six.

"This is it?" Svetla spotted the Highway 9 sign: Felton, Ben Lomond, Boulder Creek.

"Right," Morgan said, "off here."

Highway 880 was never empty. Even well after dark, it was streaked with headlights in both directions, fellow travelers oblivious to shocks and aftershocks. Tzaro felt the difference immediately as they left the exit ramp and began to climb.

At first they were following one set of taillights, but soon the car turned out of sight. The space around them, framed by firs and pines, narrowed as they climbed. The two-lane road grew darker, far from the highway lights.

"We are ... perfectly on target," Carmody interpreted the ring on Wes's screen for all of them.

"How far?" Svetla asked.

"What would you say, a mile? Less than two." The professor deferred to Wes, who had been watching the rate of zoom inside the ring.

"Less," he said. "Less than a mile now."

With the elevation and the enveloping darkness, the air that filled the car cooled, and the summer scent of the lowlands gradually modulated to a blend of evergreens, underbrush, and soil. On the gently winding road, their headlights and the glow of Wes's screen were the only illumination.

"We're close," Wes said, and Svetla let up on the gas.

"What's this?" She spotted it first and braked, a space that appeared to be a turnout on the opposite shoulder, on the uphill side.

Tzaro saw the exact image of the shoulder at the bottom of Wes's ring.

"We're here," he said.

Past the opening, a gravel road curved up the hill.

"Hawk Creek Resort." Morgan read the faded lettering on the weathered sign between wooden posts. Beyond the sign the driveway was closed with a chain, a *No Trespassing* sign suspended in the middle.

"In there?"' Clearly Svetla was hoping for a correction.

"Yes. I'm getting a location up the hill, probably at the top of that drive." Wes was interpreting the simple white triangle in the center of the ring.

Tzaro imagined sentries between them and the triangle—special forces of a rogue state or other mercenary thugs—either type with infrared scopes.

"Svetla, can you circle back?" he said. "And if you could kill your lights."

She cut left across the empty lanes, rolled over the far shoulder, and headed back with no headlamps. Moonlight or starlight barely revealed the apron of gravel. She pulled into it and stopped, an abrupt off-road rumble of stones under the tires. When she killed the engine, sudden silence. They sat until they heard crickets.

"Let's take this a step at a time," Tzaro said. "If it's clear I'll signal." His door was on the uphill side. He pushed it open and then pressed it closed softly. Outside, he realized he was, in the cool mountain air, unshielded, but possibly less than a hundred yards from the reason they had come. Forces in motion, he recalled, irreversible. He crouched, tuned like any forest animal to the earthy smell of the woods, the ticking of the cooling engine, insect chatter. He was past the front fender when the door swung open behind him.

"Go," Wilson ordered before he could object to his volunteer companion.

They trudged through blackberry and ivy around the chain post and began to pick their way through the fern and low brush off the shoulder of the gravel road. They had gone only a few yards when Tzaro spotted a frame cabin, mossy roof, windows dark. Higher up he could make out the ghostly box of another. He motioned Wilson down.

They crouched and froze, checking for any sign of motion in the cabins or the surrounding trees and brush. It crossed his mind for the first time that Quill could have been right, the enemy could be an automation, an unmanned installation left to function on its own. He tried not to be carried away by the fantasy. Nothing moving. He nodded to Wilson. They worked back within sight of the car and waved.

"So is this the HQ? What the hell *is* it?" Morgan was in the lead with her backpack. The others filled in behind her, crouching low. Wes retained his laptop strapped over his shoulder.

"Two cabins, we don't know what else," Tzaro said.

"They're deserted, right?"

He picked up on her subtext: goose chase. Instead of valuing it with an answer, he moved out first. They crept silently up the hill, the drive acquiring a filigree of creepers. For a moment Tzaro heard traffic on the road below them, but it fell silent.

"There's more." Wilson was pointing to the far side of the hill opposite the first cabins. Two others came into view, and then a third. Together they formed a semicircle, and in the center a longer frame building, green roof, sat in a clearing flanked by tall pines.

"So now do we see who's home?" Svetla joined Tzaro and the others at the front.

He spotted eyes spotting him, two then four, reddish then shiny black, just off the drive in ferns. He hoped they were not skunks, and then they were clear: a mom and a little one, shiny black eyes peering out of raccoon masks. He started to point them out to the others.

Impact, sudden and dull. A plug of bark and yellow powder erupted from a pine trunk beside Wilson. Behind them, he realized, down the hill. Only a muted pock, a silencer.

"Get down!" He shoved Morgan and Svetla into the brush and the raccoons scattered. They all crashed in and flattened against the hill in the ferns and undergrowth. In a few moments Morgan lifted her head and pointed, and Tzaro followed the line of her arm. A male figure was crouching below them on the hill, a long pistol barrel visible, the expected silencer. In the pale moonlight, he broke across the drive to their side. Tzaro noticed his gate, a subtle hitch, left foot dragging.

"Cheung," she all but gasped. "He's after me." She started to stand.

"What are you doing? Get down!" He pulled her into a crouch.

"Quill gave me a gun..."

She slipped a strap off one shoulder and swung her pack around. Adrenaline charged it with too much momentum and it slipped out of her hand. Beyond them, the slope of the hill was quicker and rugged, and Morgan's backpack glanced off rocks into a narrow ravine and rolled.

As she scrambled to retrieve it, a deafening explosion blew out of the spot on the hillside. Tzaro pulled her down flat. Rocks and vegetation scattered down the hill. Debris pelted through the leaves around them. They all lay panting under a shower of fresh dirt.

Booby-trapped. The realization fell through Tzaro, a grim confirmation that they had been right. They could trip a wire anywhere on the hill of tangled shrubs. They could not go back down. They lay in silence, pinned.

And then he heard it again, a dull thud in a tree trunk, close but unseen. Then a rip through the foliage around them. And another, closer.

CHAPTER 24   DEAD SET

Tzaro knew Cheung didn't need to fire from a distance. He could simply make his way up the drive and pick off Morgan and all of them, flat on the ground, unarmed.

They had to work away from the drive into the ravine that had taken Morgan's backpack. From there they could follow it down to the road and the car. The gully was a dark tunnel of smoke. Gunpowder smell mixed with raw earth. Tripwires could be anywhere—down the hill, or between them and the gorge.

As soon as they moved, Cheung could close on them. Even if they made it to the ravine, he would have the high ground. The gorge could be a death trap. Tzaro could not make the decision alone. He turned to Wilson.

Another blast pulverized whatever he was going to say. A gut-wrenching explosion, this time below them. Head spinning, he needed to make sense of it. Not them, not their things. Cheung's left foot.

He sat up far enough to see the smoke cloud, then started to roll to his feet.

"What are—?" Carmody caught his leg. "Tzaro!"

Wilson was standing with him.

Cheung had made it over halfway to their position. A few yards into the brush from the drive, smoke was boiling from the hill. As it began to disperse, the body emerged, front down, head lower than his feet. He could have stuck to the drive instead, Tzaro thought, but he had no way to know they weren't armed, so his fatal approach was no doubt SOP. For the first time he saw the black car at the base of the hill behind Svetla's.

"Anything?" he said.

A breath passed and then another as he and Wilson watched the body for any sign of life.

"No," Wilson said.

Morgan's and Svetla's heads came up like groundhogs. Carmody and Wes sat up.

Tzaro was feeling lightheaded. He squatted, then knelt. They had all nearly been killed. Their would-be assassin was dead below them on a rock hill in a scenario he was finding impossible to imagine.

"Everybody okay?" he forced out. Silent nods from all.

He turned to check the hill above them, especially the main building. He grabbed Wilson's shirt and tugged him down.

"They've heard us by now," he croaked, his throat a dry sleeve. "Unless there's no one up there to hear."

"We ready?" he heard himself say but it didn't sound real. He stared into the groundcover between his shoes and pulled two breaths. Cheung's explosion had been closer to the gravel than theirs, but at least ten yards into the brush. "Let's keep close to the drive."

He drove himself to his feet and his knees wobbled. They began to work their way up, taking cover as it was available fifteen feet in from the drive. They checked for any glint of moonlight on monofilament, a trace of a tripwire. Even with the moon, they were making their way in shadows, going on faith.

The first cabin Tzaro had spotted offered full cover, and he headed for it. They all flattened against the wall on the downhill side, catching their breath.

"Perhaps we could use one of these." Carmody whispered heavily. "As a base of operations."

He and Tzaro edged to the window. Old curtains bordered the frame, and the blind hung halfway down. Inside was darkness the color of dust, shadow shapes of a bed and dresser, and the clear sense of no occupancy.

"You're right, we should have a fallback position. Svetla, Morgan, I need you to stay here with the professor."

"No," Cal said, "I didn't mean me."

"Screw that," Morgan replied.

"Screw that!" Svetla echoed.

Tzaro regarded his professor who had somehow followed him into the vortex, and under the influence of that recognition and buoyed by a wave of affection, he grinned and shrugged. Around the corner of the cabin, he checked the path ahead.

"We'll lose our cover."

With the beginning of the cabins, the shoulders of the drive were broader and mostly clear of vegetation. The cabins sat in small clearings, and the only shrubs dense and tall enough to afford protection were on the perimeter. They were all looking at the next cabin.

"Ready?"

Immediately as he broke around the wall, Tzaro was in a clear line of sight of the main lodge. For long seconds they were all easy targets for any sniper behind the dark windows. A blackbird flushed squalling from the brush beyond the cabin, and Tzaro felt a jolt of panic. It carried him the last strides to the far end of the wall. The others packed in behind him, Wes and Carmody bringing up the rear.

It was the last cabin before the lodge. Two steel drums and a box freezer sat at the end of the building, and Tzaro and the others hunkered down behind them. From there they had a clear view of the lodge. A rusted iron hawk sculpture stood like a sentry in an island of brown grass in the center of the circular drive. The long lodge building, cedar plank with a green steel roof, could have been a four-star accommodation in its day. The *Keep Out* sign on the door looked official, probably municipal property condemned. The four windows on the front were rectangles of black dark. No lights visible inside. No car in the drive.

"So this is it." Tzaro was acknowledging their only conclusion but still trying to convince himself. As a base of operations, it seemed incredible. But Spear Six had the originating IP within a hundred yards of them, and the mines in the hill spoke for themselves. "Maybe it's only computers in there and we can take them down. But we can't take the chance. Just because they haven't hit us yet doesn't mean they can't. Let's check the back."

"What for?" Svetla whisper-shouted. "This place is like totally deserted. See with your own eyes. There's nothing here."

"The back route would mean less visibility," Carmody said, "to cameras or ... anyone. But it would also mean more exposure—"

"To the freaking bombs in the ground all over the place here!" Svetla finished.

"Look, I've dragged you all out here into this. I'd rather not get you all killed. I'm going the back way. It's lighter here, easier to see any tripwires. Anybody who wants to come, great. But others, please stay right here—"

"Listen, I don't know what you're saying." Morgan was hard-faced. "How did you drag me into this? I'm here for Therica, regardless of what you're making this into. I'm here because I need to be and if we're going in, I'm going in."

"If you're going, I'm going," Svetla said.

"We've come this far," Carmody added, "of our own voli-
tion."

Tzaro checked Wes.

"Wherever PUD-Z is coming from, it's here."

"We're going, boss," Wilson summarized.

Outnumbered and disarmed by support, Tzaro shook his
head and took a breath. Finally he nodded. Then he focused
on the access around the side to the rear and moved out,
keeping low.

He duck-walked, checking the bushes he was leading them
through for any spider web strand of tripwire. The end of the
building came into view—one window. He squinted to see light.

"God—!"

Behind Wilson, Svetla had caught on a root. She looked up
wince-faced, rubbing her ankle furiously. She nodded okay.

They worked the edge of the woods around the end of the
building until Tzaro could see the window clearly. His hand
went up and they froze—faint light in the room, possibly LED,
a flex-display or laptop. He locked on to the window, scanning
for any sign of motion. They waited it out, dim light and
silence.

They crept on, around the side and toward the back of the
structure which seemed larger and more ominous as they
passed closer to the woods. Taller trees interrupted the
moonlight with patches of near-total dark. In the brush behind
the building they began to inch, checking and rechecking for
tripwires, snail's progress. A loop of gravel drive continued in
the back, but they kept their distance from it, working their
way into taller sword ferns and bushes that nearly hid them at
the tree line. No vehicle was visible, but a couple of smaller
drives split off the main and trailed into the trees. Any
occupant could easily park concealed.

Tzaro surveyed the rear of the building. In the left half, two
windows, blinds lowered, framed the sides of a moss-stained
white door. At the top of the door was a glass pane, no blind.

On the right side, a concrete loading dock fronted a metal accordion door rolled down shut.

"You see a lock?" he whispered to Wilson at his side, nodding toward the metal door. Wilson squinted, shook his head.

"I don't want to take a chance with the other one, that door pane."

"The dock," Wilson said and nodded.

Tzaro understood he was ready to come too, and it felt solid and reassuring, but he fought his first reaction.

"Look, we can't take a chance here. Maybe they've been asleep at the switch, but they could pick us up anytime. Follow me but keep your cover—I'll signal if I need help. If I can get that door open, we're all in."

Wilson looked away, then back, clearly not bought in. Tzaro knew how tuned he was, and he was almost ready to reconsider, but he had said what he said.

"Okay, boss. Okay."

Tzaro whispered the plan to the others, then they moved out gingerly, Wilson following, reversing the way they had come. Soon they were even with the corner of the loading dock.

"See a camera?" Tzaro breathed, scanning what he could make out of the wall above the steel door.

After a long moment, Wilson shook his head.

A dozen or so yards of open driveway separated them from the dock. Tzaro checked Wilson, gathered himself, studied his path in the moonlight, and broke from cover.

CHAPTER 25 TRESPASS

At the edge of the dock Tzaro slapped palms on the cool concrete and hauled himself up. He scrambled to the far side of the accordion door and hunkered down beside it. The platform smelled stony and moist.

Dead end, he thought the second he spotted it—a padlock he hadn't been able to see from the ground lying flat at the corner of the door, the shackle looped through a steel eye. He tugged at it. Futile. It was an ancient key lock, no sensor. He could see rust in the keyhole.

He ran through the options. The back door where he could try to force the lock, loud and in view of the glass pane. His own keys that would be useless as lock picks. On his keychain, a wheel of screwdriver heads, each only a quarter-inch deep. He turned back to Wilson and tilted the lock up so he could see.

The Indian sat in the brush watching, as though waiting to be visited by a response. Tzaro saw his head duck down behind the thicket. Then he was up again, something in his hand Tzaro couldn't make out, a thin, white sliver in the moonlight. Suddenly he pitched it onto the landing. Tzaro scrambled the few feet to retrieve it.

Six or seven inches long, smooth and pencil-thick at one end, a light shaft of bone tapered to a point. Whalebone, Tzaro imagined. The term that crossed his mind was "pointing stick," a shaman's tool of magic to finger a victim. Wilson rotated his fist until Tzaro got it. Turning a key.

The old lock could challenge a steel key; it would macerate a needle of bone. He glanced back at Wilson, incredulous. Again he mimed turning the key.

Sure of the futility, Tzaro tilted the bottom of the lock and inserted the point. The bone ticked a pin, swiveled around it. He inserted it gingerly until it stopped.

He torqued up slightly with the expected results. The pick bowed against the steel cylinder. He checked Wilson who sat, impassive. He pulled the bone out halfway and re-inserted until it touched bottom. He jiggled it and rotated right then left.

He felt an odd sensation, like a buzzer in his hand. A nerve tweak, a jam in his wrist—split-second diagnoses. He didn't have time to decide.

The lock dropped open. Now the buzzer was in his head. And down his spine to his crotch and toes. It hadn't been locked at all—the only explanation. It had been retarded by rust and had separated when he tugged and dropped it the first time. Wilson's finger of bone had no supernatural powers. He told himself he knew that. He slipped it out.

He unhooked the shackle loop and held up the open padlock for Wilson to see. Then he turned back to the tree line where he could make out the forms of the others. He held up his palm and pushed twice, a clear *wait*.

He positioned himself in front of the door and gripped the handle. How could it not be alarmed? But the explosion on the hill had drawn no response. He checked the edges of the steel door, knowing at the same time that any sensors would be hidden in the frame. And the camera could be inside, lights on a motion sensor. Or they could have been on camera all along, the watchers only waiting. He was frozen, unable to lift the handle.

Suddenly Wilson hit the end of the platform and collected beside him. The shock of his bulk resolved into relief. Tzaro would not face what lay beyond the door alone. Wilson retrieved the bone from the landing by the lock.

"That thing..." Tzaro started but couldn't risk being heard.

Wilson said nothing but looked pleased. The bone disappeared into his cargo pants, a pocket below the knee.

Wilson's hand joined Tzaro's on the handle. They checked each other. In a moment, braced for an alarm to shriek, Tzaro nodded.

The steel rollers rattled and squeaked in the frame. An inch of dark space appeared above the concrete. Silence. They halted, panting. Resumed.

They went steadily without the luxury of inching it, both of them easy targets. When the bottom was waist height, they ducked under and slid prone on the floor.

In the dark, the room seemed dimensionless. Tzaro could not see the back wall. He made out shadowy forms of boxes on pallets, a stack of Adirondack chairs, rake and shovel handles, and between the pallets, a hand truck.

He clamped his eyes shut on a scenario of sudden lights, blinding, thugs in makeshift uniforms with AR-15s and thirty-round magazines. He tried to focus on his breath and the smell of the concrete. Wilson's head was up, surveying the room. Then he was pushing up to his knees and standing. Tzaro followed.

Nothing moved in the dark space. Quietly, deliberately, Tzaro lifted the door the rest of the way for what light there was. The left rear corner of the room came into view for the first time. He could make out a standard wooden door, no glass.

They stood together, breathing silently, tuned to any sound or sign of movement. When Tzaro was satisfied they were alone, he signaled to the others. Soon they were reunited on the platform, Svetla and Morgan first and then Carmody and Wes. Tzaro nodded toward the corner, and they tiptoed to the door in the rear.

"Want a light?" Morgan held up her phone.

"Hey, glad that wasn't in your backpack. But too risky." Tzaro felt the knob and turned, knowing already. Locked.

"Wait." Morgan fished in a pocket and traded her phone for a plastic card. She slipped it in between the door jamb and the lock and bent it toward the knob. Then, with her other hand on the knob, she bent the card back, toward the jamb, and turned at the same time. The metal tongue retracted with a click. The door cracked open and light appeared around the frame. Morgan checked the others for a moment then opened it on the room.

A hall lay before them, and beyond, the light Tzaro recognized as the emanation he had seen through the side window. They edged forward into the hallway, old dark photos on the walls of California redwoods and loggers. The corridor smelled musty from closure. As they neared the end, Tzaro motioned them to stay against the right wall, out of the line of sight.

They were close, a few steps from the end of the wall, when the light wavered. A shadow broke it. The six froze as one. The shadow was followed by a hard clack, as of a plate on granite. Then a sucking sound, slight but distinct, of a refrigerator door opening. And then a rustling of plastic, and knife and plate sounds on stone. Finally the refrigerator door was closed. The shadow was moving, breaking the light again, and there was a burst of music, factory techno. Just as suddenly, silence.

Svetla was wide-eyed, reflecting the inevitable: They were not alone, a fact they had fully anticipated but which now seemed incredible. Tzaro tried to estimate at least a minute before they risked going on. Eventually he took the first step.

At the end of the hall, they rounded the corner into the lodge kitchen, deserted, lights on. A cutting board and two plates on the counter, open chip bags, a mustard jar and cereal boxes, packs of Ramen noodles, Mountain Dew cans. Beside the sink a translucent trash bag stuffed with plastic plates and pop cans, dishes stacked there like an option exhausted before the plastic.

Tzaro could see over the kitchen counter into the old lobby of the lodge. Past the dust-colored main desk, dark leather wing chairs sat empty, paired with reading lamps with fluted shades, furnishings of a haunted hotel.

Morgan touched his arm and he nearly jumped. She pointed to the far end of the kitchen, and a door. He realized it was the one the shadow must have used. As they-cat-stepped toward it, they detected the same music, a hint at first and then clearly.

Svetla confirmed it. "They're in the basement."

Tzaro pulled one drawer and then another. He found two long knives and handed one to Wilson. The others armed themselves with knives that remained. Carmody appropriated a fire extinguisher from a closet.

They gathered again at the door and Tzaro put his ear to the wood. The same techno, rave music, but louder. As he leaned back and grasped the knob, he heard the percussion of his heart. His fingertips had left moist spots on the door. He turned the knob. The door opened on a stair, and the music welled to meet them.

CHAPTER 26 CONFLUENCE

They descended furtively, stair by stair. Tzaro had the feeling they were crossing a border between realms, entering an underwater world. As his eyes adjusted to the only light, cast by the glow of monitors, he made out half a dozen stations like office cubicles arranged in a semicircle. In the center, server boxes, blinking modems, and cables were clustered on a folding table—a hardware brain linked to the cubes by a synaptic net of wires.

In each cubicle a worker faced a screen. Even surrounded by the music that flooded the basement, they all wore headphones, which sat hugely on their heads.

Stunned, Tzaro and the others exchanged glances. The workers at the screens in oversized headphones, oblivious to the presence of invaders, were all children.

Tzaro counted three boys, two girls, middle school age or younger. Clearly they had heard nothing, not even the explosions on the hill. They existed between screen and sound, in submarine suspension, hermetically sealed.

A game flashed on one screen, bright facets and planes rotating into intersection, 3-D models, coupling assemblies. Columns of numbers, some blinking red and amber, inched up another screen. And on two, Tzaro saw the image he had sliced out of time, one in its full-color splendor, the other desaturated, a grayscale mandala, doubly sinister.

Tzaro imagined the recognition struck them all at the same time. Wilson, Carmody, and Morgan were doing what he was doing—glancing at the open double door, a dark rectangle to the adjoining room, then behind and around them. These were child labor peons of adults, who were likely to be in the building—in the basement or other rooms upstairs. But they saw no one. Tzaro took the next step.

Before they could coordinate, one of the children slipped his headphones off and rotated his chair. He started for the stairs, not looking where he was going. A few feet from them, he glanced up. His pudgy face went blank with shock. Tzaro and the others towered above him, armed with knives.

He was ten, eleven at most, stocky, in a Blastula T-shirt and baggy shorts. Tzaro snapshotted his desk—a half sandwich on a red plastic plate and an open bag of chips. He had been the shadow in the kitchen, now heading back. His chubbiness was shockingly pale, like a deep-water species.

The boy shuffled backward until he bumped another chair. A second boy swiveled to face them. Asian, a year or two older, Tzaro thought. Seeming only mildly surprised, he took a few seconds to process them then hit a key on his keyboard. The music cut to sudden silence.

The other children discovered them, turned in their chairs. They all looked like kids caught in the act—two girls, one blonde, one black, and a boy on the far end. Taller and more mature than the others, he immediately rose to his feet.

They were all suspended in silence.

"How did you do it?" The Asian boy seemed to glower at them from a pit of darkness.

Taken aback by his forthrightness, the adults were speech-less.

"What he means," the older boy said, stepping toward them seemingly without fear, "is how did you beat it? What clues?"

Tzaro was wondering how far he would go, whether the question was a ploy. He may have been thirteen, sandy-haired and tall for his age. He sounded more aggressive than the others, but he was like them in a way. He seemed altered, flat affect, curiously disengaged.

"The image," Tzaro said finally. "The clue was in the image. 1906."

"I knew it," the black girl snapped at the tall boy. "I told you that was dumb."

"Shut up!" He cupped his ears.

"Vlad," the blond girl said simply.

He quieted, took a fuming breath, sat down.

"Did someone make you do this?" Tzaro searched their faces.

They glanced at one another then turned back, avoiding eye contact. Lightless eyes.

"You know how much trouble you're in, right?" Morgan pressed.

"It was a game," the blond girl said quietly.

"Your game?"

"Yes."

"It wasn't the only idea," the Asian boy was eager to add. "We like had others. We could have done any others."

"Like messing with the grid," the pudgy one added, half-grinning.

"Did your parents—"

"No!" The black girl cut Tzaro off.

"We're not going back!" The Asian boy bolted out of his chair.

"Shut up!" Vlad was on his feet again, growling low. "Nothing about them!"

The blond girl started to whimper and the black girl left her chair to hug her. Then she looked up.

"Vlad killed her father," the black girl said simply, as though explaining she was afraid of the dark.

Tzaro felt stunned by it all, spinning when he should be making sense.

Vlad stood his ground, eyes averted, denying nothing, jaw clenched.

"He had to," the pudgy one mumbled.

"It could've been any of them," the black girl added.

"Any of your parents?" Svetla asked, unable to hide her shock.

"Vlad was the strong one," the blond girl said. "He had to be."

All of them, even Vlad, seemed immobilized in a fundamental way, as much victims as victimizers. The Asian boy rotated back to his screen, and his fingers fired nervously across the keyboard. He was resuming his game where he had paused it. One game over, Tzaro thought, another continues. A chain of games.

Wilson stepped next to Tzaro, keeping an eye on Vlad.

"What are you going to do with us?" The pudgy boy sat down, gnawing his fingernail.

The question of the hour, Tzaro understood very well. The answer depended on at least one more: What if there were others?

"Let's take a look around. And it's time for help, right?" No objections. He started to ask Morgan for her phone but spotted an old portable on one of the computer tables. He switched it on, heard a tone, and punched 911.

"We need help here. It's a complicated situation—there are a number of children involved."

The officer told him she was unable to verify his location.

"It's an old phone. We're in the Hawk Creek Resort outside Ben Lomond…it's closed…deserted except for us here.

"Really? On the way now?" The explosions, Tzaro realized. "Yes, thank you."

They would find Cheung first, he knew, but he had no time to ponder the implications. Carmody, Wes, and Morgan were in the formerly dark side room, now light, and the professor, still armed with the fire extinguisher, was waving the others over with his free hand. Svetla and Wilson volunteered to guard the children.

As Tzaro started toward the room, other lights froze him. The narrow basement windows were flashing with squad car beacons, red and white. Carmody appeared at his side, tugging him toward the room.

"Maybe he could tell us something," Wes said.

The android was the approximate height of the pudgy boy, in a Gumby T-shirt and jeans, finely featured and lifelike, a Gen 3 to Murray's 2. He stood inert, eyes downcast, in sleep mode.

"He must be their valet," Tzaro said. "Access key required, correct?"

Wes nodded.

"We'll have to interrogate—" Morgan started.

"Maybe not." Wes was opening R.B. "It's probably a four-character pin out of fifty-six thousand alphanumerics. Here's the Fire-Fi connect. This little program will try four-character combinations in sets of one hundred."

Four columns began rolling up the screen.

"There are common pins. We imagine they're random, but odds are they're human-selected, and humans, being far more alike than we are different, generate clichés. Those are flagged to bubble to the top of the sort order."

Tzaro heard tread on the floor above their heads.

"A good old binary sort," Wes mused contentedly.

They all heard a footfall at the top of the stairs.

"Police. This is the police."

"Ah," Wes said, unfazed.

The android was looking up, eyes pellucid blue, flickers of animation in its face.

"My name is Estragon. May I help you?"

CHAPTER 27   FOUNTAINHEAD

"Show me your hands! Let's see your hands!"

Four of them. The lead and his partner had Tzaro cold. Stiff arms to gunpoint, two open barrels trained on his head. Faces glistening, breathing heavily. He clenched his sphincter, flashed on St. James Episcopal, Ash Wednesday, two crosses on his forehead. In the same instant that he squeezed to maintain control, it struck him the officers had no idea what any of it was about. It was an empowering notion.

The other two officers covered Svetla and Wilson. All knives hit the floor.

Tzaro made a show of raising his hands and the others did the same, including the professor, who had migrated just outside the door. Wes hung onto R.B. but showed one open hand. Only the children remained as they were, hands in their laps or on keyboards.

The officers appeared to come from different forces. The two in the lead wore khaki—Tzaro guessed county sheriff's office. The others in blue who covered Svetla and Wilson were city cops, Santa Cruz or even Ben Lomond, if it had a department.

"Higher." The officer in charge, stone-faced, looked senior and seasoned. His tag said *SERGEANT SAZAKI*. He nodded to his female partner, tag *CONROY*, who holstered her gun and started with Tzaro, administering pat downs.

"Who can tell us what's going on here?" Sazaki was staring at Tzaro.

"There's a fatality on the hill," he began. "You must know that by now. He was an assassin. The hill is mined. Any others outside should be aware.

"There's a missing person—you should contact FBI in Seattle about that—special agent Patel.

"And there's a contagion on the web, potentially lethal. That's why we're here."

"We were about to ask some questions of our own," Carmody said. "Of an assistant, an android that accompanies the children. We really have no time to lose. You might want to join us." He continued to indulge Sazaki—hands in the air—but turned back into the side room with Wes.

Tzaro checked his officer for orders. Sazaki was fuming but letting them go. He followed as Tzaro returned to the room where the Gen 3 stirred, conscious and cordial looking. Wilson and Svetla came within earshot, still covered by the officers in blue.

Tzaro began.

"Did the children create the game?"

Estragon regarded him, clear-eyed as an honor student. "Indeed they did."

"How is that possible? How did they have the skills?"

"Fountainhead gave them special abilities." Estragon looked down, the lightest lift of a smile at the corners of his lips.

"What is Fountainhead?"

Estragon's eyes went perfectly still, no blink. Processing.

"Properties of Fountainhead ... Raw resource: youth who possess superior potential. First gateway: toddler problem solving and gaming, arithmetic. Second gateway: interdisciplinary comprehensives. Physics, biology, geometry Euclidean, geometry non-Euclidean, trigonometry, calculus. Object-oriented programming languages. Third gateway: interactive decision theory, genetic algorithms, quantum mechanics, set theory, lattice theory, metalanguages, advanced interactive decision theory. Second and third gateways are enhanced by pharmaceutical interventions. Goals: thriving, performance enhancement, mastery, superior decision-making capability."

"All lacking context," Carmody mused. "Moral, ethical, social."

"What are pharmaceutical interventions?" Tzaro went on.

"What is commonly known as 'off label' use of methylphenidate—brand names Ritalin, Metadate, Concerta—and amphetamines as performance enhancers. These in combination with mood altering medications."

Sazaki lowered his gun to his hip but kept it unholstered. "How was the instruction provided?"

"Instruction was provided by the children's parents. They selected from the Monolithic Data and aggregated the subject facets into curricula. Instructor-led classes were presented in the Magnum Caelum."

"What is that?"

"The Magnum Caelum has virtual and physical dimensions. The virtual consists of the gateways and the curricular substrate. The physical is a lyceum, a cenacle of learning, location Big Sky, Montana."

"God's country." Morgan couldn't resist but tempered her volume.

"It is a secure facility," Estragon volunteered, eyes humbly averted, a trace of a smile.

"Do you mean the children were held against their will?" Tzaro saw the android pause, and he wondered if it was calculating probabilities, weighing the implications of telling the whole truth.

"It seems that is so. They committed violence against their keepers—two are deceased. They escaped. Vladimir is a precocious driver. They chose this location for their purposes."

"What did the parents want? Why did they do this to their own children?"

"They shared an interest in pharmacology, which they referred to as a lens to expand human consciousness and a vehicle to transport emotions. They sought mastery, wealth as it can influence events, and for their offspring—the ability to shape the future as they desire."

"Power," Tzaro proposed.

"Yes."

One of the blue shirts edged into the room and held up a Ziploc to Sazaki and Conroy. It bulged with what appeared to be hundreds of capsules and pills.

Behind the officer, Tzaro saw Svetla slipping back to the children in the cubicles.

CHAPTER 28   UNDO REDO

"You might want to get all of this," Tzaro said to the sheriff's officers.

Conroy checked her chest. Her body cam light was on.

"What are the names of the children's parents, and where do they live?" Tzaro stepped to the side, allowing Conroy a direct audience with Estragon.

"Alexander Peshkov and Irina Dobritz. Last residence, Neuhausstrasse 12, Zürich, Switzerland.

"Joshua and Brittany Dierdorf. Last residence, 2014 Waverley Way, Livermore, CA.

"Kang Jung-Jin. No available last residence. Hong Kong."

With all eyes on Estragon, Tzaro slipped back into the main room where Svetla had gone. Red and white flashed in the basement windows above the other blue shirt who was searching a corner, back turned.

Svetla was with the blond girl who was rummaging in her desk drawer. As Tzaro joined them, Svetla's look implored him to keep quiet. She turned back and spoke softly.

"Holly, I need you to listen to me now, okay?"

"I'm looking for my medicine. Do you have any Adderall?"

"No. Listen, honey, is there a way to reverse it?"

Holly looked at her blankly.

"Can you reverse the effects of the game?"

She looked down, then toward her screen, rubbing the thighs of her jeans.

"That girl," she said to the screen, "the one who set her house on fire. Was it our fault?"

"Because of the game, bad things have happened to people."

She looked down at her hands, picked at a finger.

"The policeman said not to touch our computers."

"It's really important, Holly. If you know a way—"

The girl looked past Svetla, and for the first time Tzaro saw a real emotion in her eyes—fear.

"No talking to the children." The blue shirt had spotted them together and was striding to the cubicles. The other kids defaulted back to their screens like cowering students.

Tzaro sized him up. Youngster, football letter at Santa Cruz High. No idea where he was now.

"Do not touch the computers."

"Officer," Tzaro said, "this is critical. For every second—"

"Get back, please." Sazaki was directing it at Tzaro and Svetla. He and Conroy had heard from the side room. Their guns were still holstered but their hands were on the butts. Carmody, Wes, and Morgan followed behind them. "Out of this area," Sazaki growled, imperious, stone cold. "Now."

"Everything you heard in there about the game," Tzaro countered, "these kids created it. We all know what's been happening. People afraid to talk to each other, to look each other in the eye. Too paranoid to ride a bus or a train. Killing members of their own families. No motive. No cause or explanation. *This* is the cause—the game. If it can be stopped at all, these kids may be—"

"Do not touch these computers and move away from this area." Sazaki's voice boomed in the basement and his pistol was out of the holster, pointed at the floor. The kids froze at their desks. "All of this is evidence."

"Excuse me, officer… Sazaki, I believe. I have information you may want to consider." Wes sounded quietly, arrestingly calm. He was holding R.B. open before him.

"These devices are tools. They were necessary to build the game, and sustain it, but any devices would do. The object isn't these little boxes, it's the software—the game itself."

"Zen masters say," Carmody added, pointing upward, "a finger is required to point at the moon, but woe to him who mistakes the moon for his finger."

Sazaki appeared neutralized, back on his heels.

"What you should be concerned with," Wes went on, "is the server on this table. It's the hub, the physical location of the software that's running the game. Its name is an Internet protocol address, which is unique on the World Wide Web. I have it here, with the login strings provided by our Gen 3 friend. If I were to submit it to a Dark Zero site—I could do it with a few keystrokes, really—it would be locked by a Crypto Core exploitive virus that's quite impossible to block without a public key infrastructure defense on an array of machines. That isn't the configuration here. After Crypto Core runs, the contents of the server will be irretrievable without the payment of a significant ransom. It's a figure we can only guess … a ransom payment to cyberterrorists … necessitated by the decision of a single officer … of the Sheriff of Santa Cruz County."

"Sartre, Camus, a legion of our true artists and thinkers, say we may have a few, possibly only one, defining decision in a lifetime." Carmody the professor paused a moment for emphasis. "I strongly suggest you consider the opinion of our technical expert."

Red and white rotated in the windows. Tzaro was seeing Wes in cuffs, certain he would be arrested. Carmody also. Silence was stretching itself out.

"This one," Sazaki barked, pointing at Holly. "This one only."

She seemed to shrink, as though she was being called to judgment.

"It's okay, honey." Svetla squeezed her hand. "He means you can use your computer."

Holly glanced at Vlad in the next cubicle. His jaw was locked, lips tight. He took a deep breath, then nodded.

She turned to her keyboard, opened a file, and copied the contents into the mandala image. Then a wheel of dots spun once as she ran the program to post the image. In half a minute, the process was complete.

They all heard a thunder of boots in the lobby upstairs. Police backup had arrived.

"Cal, can you help us?" Tzaro knew they had seconds.

Carmody knelt beside Holly. "May I see the phrase, my dear?"

She clicked the file she had copied to the front, a few Dongba glyphs.

"Embracing peace, somewhat equivalent to the Sanskrit *shanti*. The heart-mind symbol common to mystical traditions, East and West. And the man-in-a-field character we saw before, but in triple form, representing *many* or *all*."

Tzaro heard them on the stairs.

"Peace, heart-mind, all. Peace in your heart for all." He turned to Holly.

Their eyes met and she nodded.

Tzaro waited to ask until the police woman in charge of the kids had secured them all in a single van. He and the others all had the same question.

"They'll be taken to Dominican Hospital for observation."
Her tag said *A. RICE*—a stocky black woman with a valiant
orange tint in her hair and ink on her neck. She nodded
reassuringly, and Tzaro could imagine her as their teacher, in
some other lifetime. "We don't know right now how at risk
some of them will be. They'll have to be weaned off medica-
tion." Tracks of pain, years of it, around her eyes and mouth.
Her hand was on the door handle.

"There will be an investigation to determine the status of
the parents. If they're deemed unfit by a judge, juvenile court
will keep the children in protective custody until they can be
placed, either with responsible relatives or in a supportive
environment." She nodded and Tzaro nodded. He wanted to
ask about other investigations—Montana, the international
connections, the power plot—but he could see from her
expression it was not the time.

They watched A. Rice disappear into the front of the van.
Soon they would disburse to a few of the squad cars. They had
agreed to make official statements at police headquarters in
Santa Cruz before being released. They would also have a
chance to target Sazaki with questions. The initial briefings
and coordination in the basement had taken hours. Tzaro
became aware of first light above the trees, a glow in the mist.

He felt a hand on his arm, an attention grip. Morgan was
on her phone.

"There's a message." Her expression was changing, bright-
ening. "Orcas Police … they have Therica! They found her in a
mission in Eastsound. She's on a twenty-four-hour hold. They
had instructions to call you."

Patel had made good on one promise, Tzaro thought. As
the designated contact, he returned the call on Morgan's
phone.

"I know this may sound crazy, but it's critical to do ASAP.
Log on to the Wundrus site. Stay with her while she views it,
the longer the better. I expect to be back on the island
tomorrow."

As he wound up the call, the realization struck all of them. They burst into high-fives and slapping hugs. They were safe again—Therica and Derek. All. Waves of relief tumbled through Tzaro, the curse loosening its grip, slipping, giving up with a shudder.

He had a few minutes before they would leave. Above the treetops and all around him, it felt like a new day. He crossed to the edge of the driveway, almost to the trees. Ten to six his time, ten to nine hers. The phone face glowed back at him. He was tapping the circles—six-seven-eight, eight-seven-four...

He stared into sword ferns in a pocket of mist and waited for the inevitable *number out of service*. The first ring was a shot to the heart. By the second he was starting to pray for voice mail, at the same time realizing with horror he had prepared nothing to say. And then the waiting was over.

"Hello! Rowena? It's Tzaro Janssen.

"I'm fine. Yes, it has been, definitely. How are you? Are you still in... Oh really, outside Atlanta."

He was spinning, light-headed, high on the sound of her voice.

"Yes, I've moved too, actually, outside Seattle. And divorced as well.

"Listen, I have to be heading to a meeting, and I'm sure this isn't the most convenient time for you—I just... I wanted to see if we could set a time to talk... catch up.

"Tonight would be great, yes. About eight your time? Perfect. I've been thinking..."

Tzaro looked up into the pearly brightness that seemed to be opening the sky.

"I have a lot to tell you."

EPILOGUE   One year later

Having finished her assistantship, Therica is an engineer with Evermore Geographic Ltd. in Chicago, consultants in sustainable fuel technologies.

Professor Carmody is fulfilling a series of speaking engagements on "Deciphering the Killer Code."

Morgan has settled a suit against Mesmark. With the proceeds she is buying a modular house overlooking the Point Reyes National Seashore, Marin County, California.

Wilson continues his auto repair business, specializing in the restoration of twentieth-century Volvos. He serves on the board of United Indians of All Tribes Foundation in Seattle.

Wes has taken Svetla and Holly into his home in Portland.

Svetla is enrolled in Reed College, pursuing a degree in Education. Holly helps her with her homework, and Svetla returns the favor in the spheres of fashion and romance.

Tzaro is researching school districts in Puget Sound and checking the rates of moving companies—Atlanta to Seattle.